Alfred Denis Godley

Echoes from the Oxford Magazine

Being Reprints of Seven Years. Second Edition

Alfred Denis Godley

Echoes from the Oxford Magazine
Being Reprints of Seven Years. Second Edition

ISBN/EAN: 9783337250126

Printed in Europe, USA, Canada, Australia, Japan

Cover: Foto ©Andreas Hilbeck / pixelio.de

More available books at **www.hansebooks.com**

ECHOES

FROM THE

OXFORD MAGAZINE

Oxford
HORACE HART, PRINTER TO THE UNIVERSITY

ECHOES

FROM THE

OXFORD MAGAZINE

BEING

REPRINTS OF SEVEN YEARS

SECOND EDITION

Oxford: 116 High Street
LONDON: HENRY FROWDE, AMEN CORNER, E.C.
1890

THE Poems and Parodies which make up this volume have been selected from a large number of fugitive pieces which have appeared in the columns of the OXFORD MAGAZINE since its first issue in January 1883. The following signatures may be interpreted :—

R. L. B. . R. L. BINYON, Trinity College.

C. G. F. . C. G. FAGAN, Queen's College.

A. G. . . A. D. GODLEY, Magdalen College.

S. T. . . H. W. GREENE, Magdalen College.

C. E. M. . C. E. MONTAGUE, Balliol College.

Q. . . . A. T. QUILLER-COUCH, Trinity College.

R. . . . R. W. RAPER, Trinity College.

Σ. . . . A. SIDGWICK, Corpus Christi College.

W. J. R. . R. J. WALKER, Balliol College.

F. P. W. . F. P. WALTON, Lincoln College.

CONTENTS.

CONTENTS.

A WARNING.

Addressed to the Editor of the Magazine at a time when social and educational topics were dealt with on a scale of some magnitude, and in a style of uniform sobriety.

MR. EDITOR, surely some lightness of touch
Would be not unbecoming your famed Magazine :
Of lectures and sermons you give us too much ;
Toynbee Hall gets to pall, and I loathe Bethnal
Green.

When I get my testamur, if ever I do,
And when I'm a B.A., if ever I am,
I intend, Sir, to edit a rival review,
Full of learning put lightly, like powder in jam.

My contributors almost o'erwhelm me, I own ;
The Vice-Chancellor smiles on my gallant
attempt ;
The Proctors send stories of "men they have
known,"
And the Psychicists legends of things they have
dreamt.

B

A gay sermonette full of banter and scoff
   Comes from Chichester's Dean[1], very racy and
       tart;
Mr. Page sends a leaflet on "Pulls from the off";
   Miss Broughton a novel, "A Head and his
       Heart."

I have stories of Sandford and memories of
       Merton:
   I've a new comic song—title, "Got him on toast";
I've a cryptogram, making it morally certain
   That what we call Gaius was written by Poste.[2]

Mr. Raper has promised a curious note
   On the lost compositions of writers unknown;
And the Boden Professor a tale he once wrote, [3]
   "How I shot the stuffed buffalo sitting, alone!"

There are fine Jingo projects, and Socialist dreams;
   There are Whig economics supplied me in
       shoals,
And the Russell Club send me some excellent
       schemes
   For allotments laid out in the Quad of All Souls.

[1] *Dean Burgon.*

Then the Canning and Palmerston furnish reports
  Of the speeches their members are hoping to
      make :
Norham Gardens, familiar with fashion and courts,
  Sends society gossip that's certain to take.

Such a concourse of talent makes rivalry vain :
  Though my warning is friendly, I mean what
      I 've said.
Ere we meet, Sir, as foes, let me once more
      remain
  Your respectful, admiring, but firm
                          X. Y. Z.

ΟΙΗ ΠΕΡ ΦΤΛΛΩΝ.

October's leaves are sere and wan;
    And Freshmen each succeeding year
Are, like the leaves, less verdant than
      They were.

Time was, they paced the Broad or High
    In cap and gown, with sober mien,
Their only wish to gratify
      The Dean:

But now they seek the social glass,
    The bonfire and the midnight feast:
And e'en describe their Tutor as
      A Beast.

Once, when that Tutor strove to show
    How (though it's sometimes hard to see)
There *is* a difference 'twixt οὐ
      And μή,

ΟΙΗ ΠΕΡ ΦΥΛΛΩΝ.

They gazed with simple wonder at
    The treasures of his hoarded lore,
Nor hinted that they'd "heard all *that*
        Before."

They wore a cap hind part before,
    A gown of quaint domestic cut:
They served the general public for
        A butt.

On them the casual jester tried
    (Nor failed) his old ancestral jokes:
They nightly placed their boots outside
        Their oaks.

No youths but recently from school
    Could hope to ape the senior man:
But now—I state a general rule—
        They can:

And it's comparatively rare
    For Fourth-year men, though old and gray,
To have as much of *savoir faire*
        As they.

For still among the myriad throng
   Who yearly tread Oxonia's stones
Monotony extends her sway,
And Smith grows liker every day
    To Jones.

A. G.

WILLALOO.

By E. A. P.

In the sad and sodden street,
    To and fro,
Flit the fever-stricken feet
Of the freshers as they meet,
    Come and go,
Ever buying, buying, buying
Where the shopmen stand supplying,
    Vying, vying
    All they know,
While the Autumn lies a-dying,
    Sad and low
As the price of summer suitings, when the winter
    breezes blow,
Of the summer, summer suitings that are standing
    in a row
    On the way to Jericho.

See the freshers as they row
    To and fro,
Up and down the Lower River for an afternoon
    or so—

(For the deft manipulation
   Of the never-resting oar,
Though it lead to approbation,
Will induce excoriation)—
      They are infinitely sore,
         Keeping time, time, time
         In a sort of Runic rhyme
Up and down the way to Iffley in an afternoon
            or so:
         (Which is slow).
         Do they blow?
   'Tis the wind and nothing more,
'Tis the wind that in Vacation has a tendency to go:
But the coach's objurgation and his tendency to
         "score"
      Will be sated—nevermore.

      See the freshers in the street,
         The *élite!*
   Their apparel how unquestionably neat!
   How delighted at a distance,
         Inexpensively attired,
   I have wondered with persistence
   At their butterfly existence!
         How admired!

How I envy the vermilion of the vest!
And the violet imbedded in the breast!
 As it tells,
 "This is best
To be sweetly overdressed,
 To be swells,
To be swells, swells, swells, swells,
 Swells, swells, swells,
To be simply and indisputably swells."

See the freshers one or two,
 Just a few,
 Now on view,
Who are sensibly and innocently new;
How they cluster, cluster, cluster
Round the rugged walls of Worcester!
 Book in hand,
 How they stand
In the garden ground of John's!
How they doat upon their Dons!
 See in every man a Blue!
 It is true
They are limited and lamentably few.

But I spied

Yesternight upon the staircase just a pair of
boots outside

On the floor,

Just a little pair of boots upon the stairs where
I reside,

Lying there and nothing more ;

And I swore

While these dainty twins continued sentry by
the chamber door

That the hope their presence planted should be
with me evermore,

Should desert me—nevermore.

Q.

TWILIGHT.

BY W-ll-m C-wp-r.

'Tis evening. See with its resorting throng
Rude Carfax teems, and waistcoats, visited
With too-familiar elbow, swell the curse
Vortiginous. The boating man returns,
His rawness growing with experience—
Strange union ! and directs the optic glass
Not unresponsive to Jemima's charms
Who wheels obdurate, in his mimic chaise
Perambulant, the child. The gouty cit,
Asthmatical, with elevated cane
Pursues the unregarding tram, as one
Who, having heard a hurdy-gurdy, girds
His loins and hunts the hurdy-gurdy-man
Blaspheming. Now the clangorous bell proclaims
The *Times* or *Chronicle*, and Rauca screams
The latest horrid murder in the ear
Of nervous dons expectant of the urn
And mild domestic muffin.

                              To the Parks
Drags the slow crocodile, consuming time
In passing given points. Here glows the lamp,
And tea-spoons clatter to the cosy hum
Of scientific circles. Here resounds
The football-field with its discordant train,
The crowd that cheers but not discriminates,
As ever into touch the ball returns
And shrieks the whistle, while the game proceeds
With fine irregularity well worth
The paltry shilling.—
                         Draw the curtains close
While I resume the night-cap dear to all
Familiar with my illustrated works.

                                            Q.

CARMEN GUALTERI MAP EX AUL.
NOV. HOSP.

Otiosus homo sum : cano laudes oti :
Qui laborem cupiunt procul sint remoti :
Ipse sum adversus huic rationi toti :
Pariter insaniunt ac si essent poti.

Diligens Arundinis lucidique solis,
Aciem quod ingeni acuis et polis,
Salve dium Otium, inimicum scholis
Atque rebus omnibus quae sunt magnae molis!

Nota discunt alii remigandi iura,
Qua premendus arte sit venter inter crura :
Haec est vitae ratio longe nimis dura :
Nulla nobis cutis est deterendae cura.

Habitu levissimo magna pars induto
Pellunt pilas pedibus, concidunt in luto :
Hos, si potest fieri, stultiores puto
Atque tantum similes animali bruto.

Alius contrariis usus disciplinis
Procul rivo vivit et Torpidorum vinis:
Nullus unquam ponitur huic legendi finis:
Vescitur radicibus Graecis et Latinis:

Mihi cum ut subeam Moderationes
Tutor suadet anxius "Frustra" inquam "mones:
Per me licet ignibus universas dones
Aeschyli palmarias emendationes!"

Ego insanissimos reor insanorum
Mane tempus esse qui dictitent laborum:
Otium est optimum omnium bonorum:
Ante diem medium non relinquo torum.

Ergo iam donabimus hoc praeceptum gratis
Vobis membris omnibus Universitatis,
Dominis Doctoribus, Undergraduatis—
PROFESSORES CVRA SIT OMNES VT FIATIS.

A. G.

RETROSPECTION.

After C. S. C.

WHEN the hunter-star Orion,
   (Or, it may be, Charles his Wain),
Tempts the tiny elves to try on
   All their little tricks again;
When the earth is calmly breathing
   Draughts of slumber undefiled,
And the sire, unused to teething,
   Seeks for errant pins his child;

When the moon is on the ocean,
   And our little sons and heirs
From a natural emotion
   Wish the luminary theirs;
Then a feeling hard to stifle,
   Even harder to define,
Makes me feel I'd give a trifle
   For the days of Auld Lang Syne.

James—for we have been as brothers,
   (Are, to speak correctly, twins),
Went about in one another's
   Clothing, bore each other's sins,
Rose together, ere the pearly
   Tint of morn had left the heaven,
And retired (absurdly early)
   Simultaneously at seven—

James, the days of yore were pleasant,
   Sweet to climb for alien pears
Till the irritated peasant
   Came upon us unawares ;
Sweet to devastate his chickens,
   As the well-aimed catapult
Scattered, and the very dickens
   Was the natural result ;

Sweet to snare the thoughtless rabbit;
   Break the next-door neighbour's pane ;
Cultivate the smoker's habit
   On the not-innocuous cane ;
Leave the exercise unwritten ;
   Systematically cut
Morning school, to plunge the kitten
   In his tomb, the water-butt.

Age, my James, that from the cheek of
  Beauty steals its rosy hue,
Has not left us much to speak of:
  But 'tis not for this I rue.
Beauty with its thousand graces,
  Hair and tints that will not fade,
You may get from many places
  Practically ready-made.

No ; it is the evanescence
  Of those lovelier tints of Hope—
Bubbles, such as adolescence
  Joys to win from melted soap—
Emphasizing the conclusion
  That the dreams of Youth remain
Castles that are An delusion
  (Castles, that's to say, in Spain).

Age thinks "fit," and I say "fiat."
  Here I stand for Fortune's butt,
As for Sunday swains to shy at
  Stands the stoic coco-nut.
If you wish it put succinctly,
  Gone are all our little games ;
But I thought I 'd say distinctly
  What I feel about it, James.

                                    Q.

                c

HEPHAESTUS IN OXFORD.

Ἐν δ' ἐτίθει ποταμοῖο βίην κλυτὸς ἀμφιγνήεις·
ἔνθα δύω νῆας κοῦροι ἔριδα προφέροντες
ὦκα προήρεσσον· πίσυρας δ' ἐνέθηκεν ἑκάστῃ·
ἑξῆς δ' ἑζόμενοι κρατερὸν ῥόον ὦσαν ἐρετμοῖς
τέρματος ἱέμενοι, ῥινοὶ δ' ὑπένερθεν ἔτριφθεν.
λαοὶ δ' ὡς ὅτε κῦμα πολυφλοίσβοιο θαλάσσης
θρῶσκον ἐπασσύτεροι ποταμῷ παρὰ δινήεντι,
θάρσυνον δ' ἑτάρους, ἐπὶ δ' ἴαχον ἀμφοτέροισι
θεσπεσίῳ ὁμάδῳ· ἑτέροισι δὲ φαίνετο νίκη.

 Ἐν δ' ἐτίθει μεγάλοιο πυρὸς σέλας· ἀμφὶ δὲ λαοὶ
ὀρχηθμῷ τέρπουντ' ἐρικύδεος εἵνεκα νίκης.
οἱ δ' ἐπεὶ οὖν πόσιος καὶ ἐδητύος ἐξ ἔρον ἔντο
νυκτὸς ἔπειτ' ὠρχεῦντο μέσῳ περικάλλεος αὐλῆς,
τυκτῷ ἔνι δαπέδῳ, περὶ δὲ φρένας ἤλυθεν οἶνος,
ἐν πυρὶ βάλλοντες κτῆσιν μέγαλ' ἤλιθα πολλὴν
μάψ, ἀτάρ οὐ κατὰ κόσμον· ἔπειτα δέ τ' ἔνθορον αὐτοί.
τοὺς δ' ἄρα νισσομένους ἀπ' ἀμύμονος ὀρχηθμοῖο
πρώκτωρ δέγμενος ἦστο, πέλωρ ἀθεμίστια εἰδώς,

*+ A literally true description of the revels at
Magdalen after the victory, then "fun".*

παρ ὁδῷ ἐν σκοπιῇ, ὅθι περ νίσσεσθαι ἔμελλον
[οὐκ οἶος· ἅμα τῷ γε κύνες πόδας ἀργοὶ ἕποντο].
ὡς ὁ μὲν ἐσκοπίαζ᾽, οἱ δ᾽ ἤλυθον ἀφραδίῃσιν·
δὴ τότ᾽ ἔπειτ᾽ ἐπόρουσε, γένος δ᾽ ἐρέεινεν ἑκάστου,
θωὴν δ᾽ αὖτ᾽ ἐπέθηχ᾽· οἱ δ᾽ οὐκ ἐθέλοντες ἔτινον·
ἄλλοι δ᾽ ἄλλοσ᾽ ἔφευγον ἀνὰ τρηχεῖαν ἀταρπόν.

A. G.

IN A COLLEGE GARDEN.

Senex. Saye, cushat, callynge from the brake,
         What ayles thee soe to pyne?
     Thy carefulle heart shall cease to ake
         Ere spring incarnadyne
         The buddynge eglantyne :
         Saye, cushat, what thy griefe to myne?

Turtur. Naye, gossip, loyterynge soe late,
         What ayles thee thus to chyde?
     My love is fled by garden-gate ;
         Since Lammas-tyde
         I wayte my bryde.
         Saye, gossyp, whom dost thou abyde?

Senex. Loe! I am he, the "Lonelie Manne,"
         Of Time forgotten quite,
     That no remembered face may scanne—
         Sadde eremyte,
         I wayte tonyghte
         Pale Death, nor any other wyghte.

O cushat, cushat, callynge lowe,
  Goe waken Time from sleepe:
Goe whysper in his ear, that soe
    His besom sweepe
    Me to that heape
  Where all my recollections keepe.

Hath he forgott? Or did I viewe
  A ghostlie companye
This even, by the dismalle yewe,
    Of faces three
    That beckoned mee
  To land where no repynynges bee?

O Harrye, Harrye, Tom and Dicke,
  Each lost companion!
Why loyter I among the quicke,
    When ye are gonne?
    Shalle I alone
  Delayinge crye "Anon, Anon"?

Naye, let the spyder have my gowne,
  To brayde therein her veste.
My cappe shal serve, now I "goe downe,"
    For mouse's neste.
    Loe! this is best.
  I care not, soe I gayne my reste.
                                    Q.

A FRAGMENT.

With apologies to AESCHYLUS *and* MISS EDGEWORTH.

'Απῴχετ' οὖν ἐς κῆπον, ὡς ἀποσχίσαι
φυλλεῖα κράμβης, μήλινον τεῦξαι γάνος·
δεινὴ δ' ἐπῆλθεν ἄρκτος, ἐν μέσῃ θ' ὁδῷ
κάρα προκύψασ' ἐς τὸ κουρεῖον βοᾷ·
Τί γάρ; κονίας ἆρ' ἔχει σ' ἀχηνία;
ὁ δ' οὖν ἀπώλεθ'· ἡ δ' ἀπρόσκοπος κακοῦ
κῆδος ξυνῆψε τῷ ξύρων ἐπιστάτῃ.
ἧκον δ' ἐς ἑστίασιν οἱ Γωβλίλλιοι
χοἰ Γαρίουλοι, Πευκανινίων 'τ' ὄχλος,
ὑπέρτατόν τε θρέμμα, Παγγάνδρου βία,
σμικρὸν κυκλοῦντα θριγκὸν ἐξηρτυμένος.
ἐς παιδιὰν δὲ πᾶς μετεστράφη λεώς,
ἄλλοι παρ' ἄλλων ὡς τύχοι δεδεγμένοι,
ἕως ἀπ' ἄκρας ἀρβύλης ἐσπαρμένη
εἰκῇ διῇσσεν ἀστραπηφόρος κόνις.

Σ.

ANECDOTE FOR FATHERS.

Designed to show that the practice of lying is not confined to children.

BY THE LATE W. W. (OF H. M. INLAND REVENUE SERVICE).

AND is it so? Can Folly stalk
And aim her unrespecting darts
In shades where grave Professors walk
    And Bachelors of Arts?

I have a boy, not six years old,
A sprite of birth and lineage high:
His birth I did myself behold,
    His caste is in his eye.

And oh! his limbs are full of grace,
His boyish beauty past compare:
His mother's joy to wash his face,
    And mine to brush his hair!

One morn we strolled on our short walk,
With four goloshes on our shoes,
And held the customary talk
    That parents love to use.

(And oft I turn it into verse,
And write it down upon a page,
Which, being sold, supplies my purse
  And ministers to age.)

So as we paced the curving High,
To view the sights of Oxford town
We raised our feet (like Nellie Bly),
  And then we put them down.

"Now, little Edward, answer me"—
I said, and clutched him by the gown—
"At Cambridge would you rather be,
  Or here in Oxford town?"

My boy replied with tiny frown
(He'd been a year at Cavendish),
"I'd rather dwell in Oxford town,
  If I could have my wish."

"Now, Edward, tell me why 'tis so;
My little Edward, tell me why."
"Well, really, Pa, I hardly know."
  "Remarkable!" said I:

"For Cambridge has her 'King's Parade,'
And much the more becoming gown;
Why should you slight her so," I said,
  "Compared with Oxford town?"

At this my boy hung down his head,
While sterner grew the parent's eye;
And six-and-thirty times I said,
  "Why, Edward, tell me why?"

For I loved Cambridge (where they deal—
How strange!—in butter by the yard);
And so, with every third appeal,
  I hit him rather hard.

Twelve times I struck, as may be seen
(For three times twelve is thirty-six),
When in a shop the *Magazine*
  His tearful sight did fix.

He saw it plain, it made him smile,
And thus to me he made reply:—
"*At Oxford there's a Crocodile*[1];
  And that's the reason why."

Oh, Mr. Editor! My heart
For deeper lore would seldom yearn,
Could I believe the hundredth part
  Of what from you I learn.

                       Q.

[1] *Obscure allusions to a crocodile, kept at the Museum, had been perplexing the readers of the Magazine for some time past, and had been distorted into an allegory of portentous meaning.*

D. T. FABULA;

OR, PLAIN LANGUAGE FROM TRUTHFUL JAMES [1].

Do I sleep? Do I dream?
   Am I hoaxed by a scout?
Are things what they seem,
   Or is Sophists about?
Is our τὸ τί ἦν εἶναι a failure,
   Or is Robert Browning played out?

Which expressions, though strong,
   Are μείωσις (or mild
As the Warden's Souchong)
   To the words of this child
When he sees a Society busted,
   Or otherwise sp'iled.

'Twas December the third,
   And I said to Bill Nye,
"Which it's true what I've heard,
   If you're, so to speak, fly,
There's a chance of some Tea and tall
   Culture—
The sort they call 'High.'"

[1] *The Oxford Browning Society expired at Keble the week before this was written.*

Which I mentioned its name,
  And he ups and remarks,
"If dress coats is the game
  And pow-wow in the Parks,
I'm nuts on the Rabbi Ben Ezra,
  The same I call larks."

But the pride of Bill Nye
  Cannot well be expressed;
For he wore a white tie
  And a cut-away vest.
Says I, "Solomon's lilies ain't in it,
  And *they* were well-dressed."

But not far did we wend
  When we met an old Don,
Who was sobbing no end,
  With his Sunday-best on:
And he groaned and said "Busted, by Jingo!"
  And then he was gone.

And I said, "This is odd";
  But we came pretty quick
To a sort of a quad
  That was all of red brick:
And I said to the Porter, "R. Browning,
  And kindly look slick."

But he looked on Bill Nye,
    And he looked upon me;
And the gleam in his eye
    Was quite dreadful to see.
Says he, "The Society's busted,
    Which some say it's Tea."

Then we took off our coats,
    Showed our sleeves (which were b'iled),—
Which the same it denotes
    That a party is riled,—
And we went for that man, till his mother
    Had doubted her child.

But I ask, Do I dream?
    Am I hoaxed by a scout?
Are things what they seem,
    Or is Sophists about?
Is our τὸ τί ἦν εἶναι a failure,
    Or is Robert Browning played out?

                            Q.

CALIBAN UPON RUDIMENTS[1];

OR, AUTOSCHEDIASTIC THEOLOGY IN A HOLE.

RUDIMENTS, Rudiments, and Rudiments!
'Thinketh one made them i' the fit o' the blues.

'Thinketh, one made them with the "tips" to match,
But not the answers; 'doubteth there be none,
Only Guides, Helps, Analyses, such as that:
Also this Beast, that groweth sleek thereon,
And snow-white bands that round the neck o' the
      same.

'Thinketh, it came of being ill at ease.
'Hath heard that Satan finds some mischief still
For idle hands, and the rest o 't. That's the case.
Also 'hath heard they pop the names i' the hat,
Toss out a brace, a dozen stick inside;
Let forty through and plough the sorry rest.

'Thinketh, such shows nor right nor wrong in them,
Only their strength, being made o' sloth i' the
      main—

[1] *Caliban museth of the now extinct Examination in the Rudiments of Faith and Religion.*

'Am strong myself compared to yonder names
O' Jewish towns i' the paper. Watch th' event—
'Let twenty pass, 'have a shot at twenty-first,
'Miss Ramoth-Gilead, 'take Jehoiakim,
'Let Abner by and spot Melchizedek,
Knowing not, caring not, just choosing so,
As it likes me each time, I do : so they.

'Saith they be terrible : watch their feats i' the Viva !
One question plays the deuce with six months' toil.
Aha, if they would tell me ! No, not they !
There is the sport : "come read me right or die ! "
All at their mercy,—why they like it most
When—when—well never try the same shot twice !
'Hath fled himself and only got up a tree.

     *   *   *   *   *   *

'Will say a plain word if he gets a plough.

                                       Q.

CHAUCER IN OXENFORDE.

At Oxenforde I sawe in that citee
of yongë clerkes a ful gret compagnie,
and I wol nowe you tellen everich on
hir wone and eke of hir condicioun.

An aesthete was there as I schell you tell,
that hadde of artë lernèd every del;
of Michael-Ange and Raffael and Giote
he couldë glosen of hem al by rote.
Sober his eyen were and holwe and sad,
and streyte broun hayre and somdel long he had,
and smylede wearily as he wolde say
"this is a sorry Age now by my fay."
His cote and hatte were al of olive broun,
and faste he steppède as about the toun
and schort and quicke, and lokède fixedly
as if these lewdë folk he mowght nat see;
but in the feldës on a May morning
he woldë here the smalë foulës sing,

and ydle ther for hourës nine or twelve,
makinge of littel songés for himselve.
He walkède on his toon ful deintily
as if his botës pynched him privily.
Of flesche on him ther was no ferthing sene,
yet natheles he woldë ben more lene,
for to be fleschlich is a dedly synne,
and al his lust was for to growe more thynne.
He lokède so for-pined that I upsterte
and saidë, "Frend, come telle me al thy herte,
thou art y-famischèd, it is no drede,
take here a grote thy porë corps to fede ;
ete now a joly roost or elles a stew :
thise littel deinty pottës white and blew
wol not suffice : they bin not servisable ;
I schall thee make to sitten attë table
and drinken ale and ete a roostë joynt :
thou schalt be fat, pardý, and in good poynt."
But he ne spake, but left me ther I stood ;
he was a hautein man by Christës blood.
The porë peple gapèd him upon,
and sothely twas no wonder by Saint John !

A Schipman was there eke, a bote captáin,
that woldë souffre mochel toil and payne

teachand the freschĕ clerkes howe to rowe;
thise straungĕ cries bin all to him y-knowe
which that they usen by the stremĕs brinke,
and in the race a belle he woldĕ clinke,
ther was no clerkĕ colde more noisē make;
he was a right schipman, I undertake.
But if to souper you sholde bidde him come
he spak no mo than as if he were dumbe,
he woldĕ nothinge do but drinke and ete,
for of his talkinge he was ful discrete;
he lokède wise of countenance, pardý:
smoken he colde with grete solempnitee.
He woldĕ hearken al you scholde him tel
as he could understonden every del;
he lokède as his thoughte was grave and ful,
but wel I knewe he was an oldĕ bul
and hadde of man only the résemblaunce;
therfor folk made of him gret confiaunce.
Flaunelled he was upon his leggĕs thikke
and schuldrĕs brode; by Godde he was no stikke;
big was his brawn, I guesse, and in gret fors,
he coldĕ ete as much as doth an hors.

C. G. F.

D

A SONG OF DEGREES.

*On a proposal to extend the Statute respecting the conferring of
Degrees in absence.*

THERE's reality, then,
   In what rumours allege,
And the Council again
   Are essaying the edge
Of their ancient and dangerous weapon—once more
   the Thin End of the Wedge.

They've a scheme to propose
   (On the plan " Do ut des ")
Which will multiply those
   Who proceed to Degrees :—
You may get your M.A. from the Bursar, on sending
   the requisite fees !

We, who still have defied
   The Hebdomadal's nods,
Who have fought and have died
   (So to speak) against odds,
Who have grappled with Letto-Slavonic, and pul-
   verised History Mods—

Thus to tout for M.A.'s
    Is a thing we detest :
'Twere a standing disgrace
    If we e'er acquiesced
In a change that is simply and solely designed to
    replenish the Chest.

If Degrees don't come in
    As they used long ago,
And it's found that the tin
    In the Cashbox is low,—
Let them sell the Museum to Keble—abolish a
    Reader or so :

Let them lurk in the Corn
    After Union debates :
Let them prowl until morn
    By the Theatre's gates :
Let them proctorise golfers from Cowley, and men
    coming up from the Eights.

But your scout (as you see)
    If you simply go down
And receive your Degree
    In the Highlands—in Town—
Cannot wait at the Apodyterium, and be tipped for
    presenting your gown.

Pause, O Vice, for a while,
   And reflect, if you can,
How the system must rile
   That respectable man,
When he finds his legitimate profits reduced by
      your Radical plan.

Do I sleep? Do I dream?
   No, I fear there's no doubt
Of the truth of the scheme
   That the Council's about:
To enrich an effete institution they risk the receipts
      of the scout!

                            A. G.

MISERERE SVFFRAGATORIS.

Nunc Parvisa canamus: amant Parvisa Camenae.
ille ego, qui triplici signatam nomine chartam
iamdudum repeto—nec me labor ille iuvabat—
en, ego praeterii: nil mi gravis ante nocebat
algebra, grammaticoque carent errore papyri.
nec scripsisse satis: Vice Cancellarius ipse
haud facilem esse viam voluit, vivaque rogari
voce iubet pueros. Vidi, qui nota rogati
obstipuere tamen, meliusve tacenda loquuntur.
ipse nihil timui—quid enim rationis egerem,
sede sedens solita?—nec non cum laude recessi.

TVM ILLE RESPONDEBIT ET DICET:

Ergo ne pete plura: sit hic tibi finis honorum:
crede mihi, satis est unum Testamur habere.
fortunate puer, tua si modo commoda noris,
quod tibi iudicium suffragia rursus ademit
iam data: quod curvo terret Moderator aratro,
nec cepisse gradum, necdum licet esse magistro.

te non ulla movet facundia municipalis
trinave cum propria promittens iugera vacca
Fyffius exercet : te non ciet Hebdomadale
concilium, duplicique vocat revocatque flagello,
res quaecunque agitur :—qua sint ratione legendi
Procuratores : an sit scribenda Latine
prosa mathematicos puero qui quaerit honores :
nec tua Palgravius nec Sacri Carminis auctor
quarto quoque die poscit suffragia Dixon.

EXPLICIT DIALOGVS.   A. G.

SUFFRAGIA] 'Hoc est jus suffragandi pro membris municipalibus : quod erat privilegium admodum lucrativum, quia semicoronae et interdum pluris suffragia venditabant. Hoc jus concessum est undergraduatis, verum mox ademtum.'   MANUT.

FYFFIUS] 'Urbem repraesentare voluit. Liberales autem omnes trina aliena jugera et alienam vaccam singulis pauperibus promittebant : quae erat causa, cur liberales vocarentur.'   SCHOL.

PROCURATORES] Permittebatur Collegiis ut invicem secundum certum ordinem unum e sociis propter foeditatem morum juvenibus laniandum obicerent. Hic est cyclus qui Procuratorius vocabatur. Errant autem, qui cum hoc cyclo corpus illud cyclistarum conjungunt, quod Universitatem postea infamavit.

PALGRAVIUS] Hic enim et Dixon professoriam Poetriae cathedram petebant. Sacrum autem carmen quale fuerit, non liquet. Erant in Academia multa profana carmina, et praecipue illud, de quo antiquitus sancitum invenimus NE SACRVM ESTO NEV DICATVM IN DEORVM LAVDEM : unde Newdigatum postea appellabatur.

SOLVITUR ACRIS HIEMPS.

My Juggins, see : the pasture green,
  Obeying Nature's kindly law,
Renews its mantle; there has been
      A thaw.

The frost-bound earth is free at last,
  That lay 'neath Winter's sullen yoke
'Till people felt it getting past
      A joke;

And now the Fresher feels the sun
  And gets himself another vest,
Wherein attired, he seems as one
      Possessed.

Again the stream suspects the keel ;
  Again the shrieking captain drops
Upon his crew; again the meal
      Of chops

Divides the too-laborious day;
  Again the Student sighs o'er Mods,
And prompts his enemies to lay
    Long odds.

Again the shopman spreads his wiles;
  Again the organ-pipes, unbound,
Distract the populace for miles
    Around.

Then, Juggins, ere December's touch
  Once more the wealth of Spring reclaim,
Since each successive year is much
    The same;

Since too the monarch on his throne
  In purple lapped and frankincense,
Who from his infancy has blown
    Expense,

No less than he who barely gets
  The boon of out-of-door relief,
Must see desuetude,—then let's
    Be brief.

At those resolves last New Year's Day
  The kindly gods indulgent wink.
Then downward, ho !—the shortest way
    Is drink.

Q.

DOCTRINAE SEDES.

WHEN Pleasure rules in Learning's realm
  With Heads of Houses to escort her:
And Youth directs an errant helm
  In shorts that every year grow shorter:
When Scholars "have their People Up"
  (A plea that everything excuses),
And quaff the gay convivial cup
  Where once they wooed the classic Muses:

When men who used to come at nine
  Allege (at ten) "indisposition,"
And Brown has several aunts to dine
  And cannot do his composition:
When Tomkins—once a studious lad—
  "Desires most humbly to express a
Sincere regret he has not had
  Time to complete his weekly essay":

When Lecturers have lost their use,
  Because the youth they idly prate to
Has other things whereon to muse
  Than mere Thucydides or Plato—

(You think, perhaps, he's taking notes?
  Mistaken dream! too well I know he
Is speculating on the boats,
  Or thinking of a rhyme to Chloe):—

Then seek with me some calmer scene
  Where wines are hushed, where banjoes mute
      are;
There—careless, though they burn the Dean
  And immolate the Senior Tutor—
I'll muse in solitude, until
  June and the Long once more disbands 'em;
Then, William, pay my washing bill
  And call at once my usual hansom.

                        A. G.

ΤΩι ΒΑΚΧΩι.

Κάπνισσάν τε κατὰ κλισίας καὶ δεῖπνον ἕλοντο.—HOMER.

The earliest Pipe of half-awakened Birdseye.—TENNYSON.

Fumabat ad aras.—VERGIL.

'Ω χαῖρε Σῦριγξ, μηχάνημα Πανικόν,
τέχνην μαθοῦσα Πανικῆς ὑπερτέραν·
ὦ θεῖε Καπνέ, Νικοτίνιον γάνος,
δωρημάτων ἄριστον, εὐωδέστατον·
ὦ πημονῆς ἰατρέ, συλλῆπτορ χαρᾶς,
ἀναπνοὴ πονοῦσι, διψώντων ποτόν,
ῥιγῶσι θάλπος, καυμάτων παραψυχή,
πείνῃ φθίνουσιν ἑστίασις εὐτελής·
πῶς δὴ τοσούσδ' αἰῶνας ἀνθρώπων γένος
χρείαν ἔχον σοῦ λανθάνεις τοιοῦτος ὤν;
ἢ πόλλ' ἐρημίαισιν 'Αλπειναῖς ἁλούς,
παύροις ἑταίροις συμπλακεὶς ἐν ὁρμαθῷ,
σπαρτοῦ λαβόμενος, βαρβάρων ἡγουμένων,
κρυσταλλοπλῆγα χερσὶν ἀξίνην φέρων,
δύσπνους ἀνεῖρπον τὴν νιφόστρωτον πλάκα·
κἄπειτ', ἐπειδὴ τῆς ἄκρας βαρυστονῶν
κατήνυσ', εἴθ' ἑλκόμενος εἴτ' ἄρ' οὖν βάδην,

οἵως ἀνέπνευσ', ἐν πέτραισιν ὕπτιος
σοῖς ἀμβρότοισι νέφεσι πᾶν θέλγων κέαρ.
κοὐκ ἐν πόνοισι μοῦνον εὐφραίνεις παρών·
οὐχ ἧσσον, ἡνίκ' ἀργίας ἡσσημένος
κεῖμαι παρὰ ῥείθροισι νηνέμου θέρους,
βαφῇ τ' ὀνηθείς, ἀρτίως λελουμένος,
ἄρθροισι πίνω ψῦχος εὐθαλοῦς χλόης,
τὴν σὴν ἀνῆψα, θριγκὸν ἡδονῆς, πυράν.
μέσων δὲ νυκτῶν, εἴτ' ἀπειρηκὼς κυρῶ
δέλτοις ἀνηνύτοισιν, ἃς κρίνειν με δεῖ,
μίλτον θ' ὑφέλκειν γραμμάτων ἁμαρτίαις,
κἀπαξιοῦντα σημάτων πλῆθος νέμειν·
εἴτ' οὖν σοφοῖσι τοῖς πάλαι βαρύνομαι,
Θουκυδίδου πλοκαῖσι, Σοφοκλέους τέχνῃ,
ἀνειμένοις λόγοισι τοῖς Εὐριπίδου,
ἰδέαις Πλατωνικαῖσι, Πινδάρου δόλῳ,
χορῶν στροφαῖσιν ἐμφόβως ἐφθαρμέναις,
ἀθεσφάτοισι Τευτόνων εἰκάσμασιν,
καὶ δυσκρίτοισι φιλολόγων ὀνείρασιν,
ἰλιγγιώντων ἐν πλάνοις ἀμηχάνοις
ἀκραντομύθου σκέψεως Ὁμηρικῆς·
τοίοις πόνοισιν εὖτ' ἂν ἐκμαινώμεθα,
ὦ τρῆμα θεῖον, ὦ βροτῶν Σῦριγξ ἄκος,
ὡς σοῖσι βωμοῖς θυμίαμ' ἀνάπτομεν

τῆς σῆς θ᾽ ὀμίχλης χαίρομεν γεγευμένοι.

ἐνεγκάτω τις πῦρ βρυαντομαϊκόν,

(καῦσαι δ᾽ ἀδύνατον μὴ οὐχὶ πρὸς κίστῃ τριβέν),

λαβών τ᾽ ἄριστον καὶ μελάντατον κύτος,

καὶ Περσικαῖσιν ὑποδεδεμένος ἐμβάσιν,

κλίνῃ τε κάμψας κῶλα μαλθακωτάτῃ,

σύριγγα φλέξω, πόδας ἔχων πρὸς ἑστιάν,

καὶ πᾶν βρότειον ἐξαπαλλάξω κακόν.

Σ.

AS I LAYE A-DREAMYNGE.

As I laye a-dreamynge, a-dreamynge, a-dreamynge,
O softlye moaned yͤ dove to her mate within yͤ tree,
    And meseemed unto my syghte
    Came rydynge many a knyghte
    All cased in armoure bryghte
        Cap-à-pie,
As I laye a-dreamynge, a goodlye companye!

As I laye a-dreamynge, a-dreamynge, a-dreamynge,
O sadlye mourned yͤ dove, callynge long and call-
        ynge lowe,
    And meseemed of alle that hoste
    Notte a face but was yͤ ghoste
    Of a friend that I hadde loste
        Long agoe.
As I laye a-dreamynge, oh, bysson teare to flowe!

As I laye a-dreamynge, a-dreamynge, a-dreamynge,
O sadlye sobbed yͤ dove as she seeméd to dyspayre,

And laste upon ye tracke
Came one I hayled as "Jacke!"
But he turnéd mee his backe
With a stare:
As I laye a-dreamynge, he lefte mee callynge there.

Stille I laye a-dreamynge, a-dreamynge, a-dream-
ynge,
And gentler sobbed' ye dove as it eased her of her
payne,
And meseemed a voyce y^t cry'd—
"They shall ryde, and they shall ryde
'Tyll ye truce of tyme and tyde
Come agayne!
Alle for Eldorado, yette never maye attayne!"

Stille I laye a-dreamynge, a-dreamynge, a-dream-
ynge,
And scarcelye moaned ye dove, as her agonye was
spente:
"Shalle to-morrowe see them nygher
To a golden walle or spyre?
You have better in y^r fyre,
Bee contente."
As I laye a dreamynge, it seem'd smalle punyshment.

But I laye a-wakynge, and loe ! yᵉ dawne was break-
        ynge
And rarelye pyped a larke for yᵉ promyse of yᵉ daye :
    "Uppe and sette yʳ lance in reste !
    Uppe and followe on yᵉ queste !
    Leave yᵉ issue to bee guessed
        At yᵉ endynge of yᵉ waye"—

As I laye a-wakynge, 'twas soe she seemed to say—
    "Whatte and if it alle bee feynynge ?
    There be better thynges than gaynynge,
    Better pryzes than attaynynge."
        And 'twas truthe she seemed to saye.
Whyles the dawne was breakynge, I rode upon my
        waye.

Q.

ODE TO THE TEMPORARY BRIDGE
AT OSNEY.

Osney Bridge fell into the river and was left there by the caution of the civic authorities for about three years: its place being taken by an elegant but insecure wooden structure. This is a standing refutation of those who allege that Oxford is too prone " stare super antiquas vias."

PROUD monument of British enterprise !
   Stately highway of Commerce ! thou art old :
Since with enraptured gaze we saw thee rise
     Three winters o'er thy perilous planks have
       rolled,
Each with its load of carriages and carts :
Freshmen, who saw thy birth, are Bachelors of
       Arts.

Majestic arch, that spans the Isis' flow,
   Fraught with the memory of our lives imperilled,
We could not hope to keep thee—thou must go.
   Yet shall no bard in Chronicle or Herald,
No civic Muse, deplore thee ? none of all
Who paid augmented rates to rear thee, mourn
       thy fall ?

Thou art of schemes municipal the symbol,
  As crazy, and as tortuous.   Fare thee well!
Not long o'er thee shall Undergraduate nimble
  Evade the Proctor and his bulldogs fell:
Business and Pleasure to their old forgotten
Path will return again, and leave thy timbers
    rotten.

Perchance some Alderman, or Member of
  The Local Board,—his shallop softly mooring,—
Beside thy site contemplative will rove
  And weep awhile thy glories unenduring:
And unimpeded by thy barring wood
Dead cats and dogs shall float adown the central
    flood.
                                        A. G.

KENMARE RIVER.

'TIS pretty to be in Ballinderry,
　'Tis pretty to be in Ballindoon,
But 'tis prettier far in County Kerry
　Coortin' under the bran' new moon.
　　　　　Aroon, Aroon!

'Twas there by the bosom of blue Killarney
　They came by the hundther' a-coortin' me;
Sure I was the one to give back their blarncy,
　And ivery man in the I. R. B.

But niver a stip in the lot was lighter
　An' divvle a boulder among the bhoys,
Than Phelim O'Shea, me dynamither,
　Me illigant arthist in clock-work toys.

'Twas all for love he would bring his figgers
　Of iminent statesmen, in toy machines,
An' hould me hand as he pulled the thriggers
　An' blew the thraytors to smithereens.

An' to see the Queen in her Crystial Pallus
    Fly up to the roof, an' the windeys broke!
And all with divvle a thrace of malus,—
    But he was the bhoy that enjoyed his joke!

Then   oh!   but   his   cheek   would   flush,   an'
    " Bridget "   .
(He'd say) "will yez love me?" But I'd be coy,
And answer him, "Arrah, now dear, don't fidget!"
    Though at heart I loved him, me arthist bhoy!

One night we stood by the Kenmare river,
    An' "Bridget, creina, now whist," said he,
"I'll be goin' to-night an' maybe for iver,
    Open your arms at the last to me."

An' there by the banks of the Kenmare river,
    He tuk in his hands me white, white face,
An' we kissed our first an' our last for iver—
    For Phelim O'Shea is disparsed in space.

'Twas pretty to be by blue Killarney,
    'Twas pretty to hear the linnet's call,
But whist! for I cannot attind their blarney
    Nor whistle in answer at all, at all.

For the voice that he swore 'ud out-call the linnet's
  Is cracked intoirely, an' out of chune,
Since the clock-work missed it by thirteen minutes
  An' scatthered me Phelim around the moon.
                    Aroon, Aroon !

                                   Q.

TO MY PAPERKNIFE.

Thou art old, my Paperknife, old and dented!
Yet hast served me well, since in Eighteen-sev'nty
I first saw thee, left in the railway-carriage,
    Left by a maiden,
Who, beside her mother demurely seated,
Glanced in turn at Telegraph, Times and Standard,
Or, above the Telegraph, Times or Standard,
    Let a look wander
Shyly forth 'neath eyelashes long and raven.
She, the unknown, alighted, but thee she left there,
Paperknife! Since then thou hast cut the leaves of
    Homer and Virgil,
Lycophron, Sidonius Apollinaris,
Rhodian Apollonius, Egyptian Hermes,
Hegel and the twain Metamorphosistae,
    Darwin and Ovid.
                  W. J. R.

THE INNINGS.

DEDICATED TO WALT WHITMAN.

I.

To take your stand at the wicket in a posture of
   haughty defiance:
To confront a superior bowler as he confronts
   you:
To feel the glow of ambition, your own and that
   of your side:
To be aware of shapes hovering, bending, watching
   around—white-flannelled shapes—all eager, unable to catch you.

2.

The unusually fine weather,
The splendid silent sun flooding all, bathing all in
   joyous evaporation.
Far off a gray-brown thrush warbling in hedge or
   in marsh;
Down there in the blossoming bushes, my brother
   what is it that you are saying?

3.

To play more steadily than a pendulum; neither hurrying nor delaying, but marking the right moment to strike.

4.

To slog :

5.

The utter oblivion of all but the individual energy :

The rapid co-operation of hand and eye projected into the ball ;

The ball triumphantly flying through air, you too flying.

The perfect feel of a fourer !

The hurrying to and fro between the wickets : the marvellous quickness of all the fields :

The cut, leg hit, forward drive, all admirable in their way ;

The pull transcending all pulls, over the boundary ropes, sweeping, orotund, astral :

The superciliousness of standing still in your ground, content, and masterful, conscious of an unquestioned six ;

The continuous pavilion-thunder bellowing after each true lightning stroke ;

(And yet a mournful note, the low dental murmur
    of one who blesses not, I fancied I heard
    through the roar
In a lull of the deafening plaudits;
Could it have been the bowler? or one of the
    fields?)

6.

Sing on, gray-brown bird, sing on! now I under-
    stand you!
Pour forth your rapturous chants from flowering
    hedge in the marsh,
I follow, I keep time, though rather out of breath. '

7.

The high perpendicular puzzling hit: the consequent
    collision and miss: the faint praise of "well
    tried."
The hidden delight of some and the loud dis-
    appointment of others.

8.

But, O bird of the bursting throat, my dusky demon
    and brother,
Why have you paused in your carol so fierce from
    the flowering thorn?

Has your music fulfilled the she-bird ? (it cannot
    have lulled her to sleep :)
Or see you a cloud on the face of the day unusually
    fine ?

9.

To have a secret misgiving :
To feel the sharp sudden rattle of the stumps from
    behind, electric, incredible :
To hear the short convulsive clap, announcing all
    is over.

10.

The return to the pavilion, sad, and slow at first :
    gently breaking into a run amid a tumult of
    applause ;
The doffing of the cap (without servility) in be-
    coming acknowledgment ;
The joy of what has been and the sorrow for what
    might have been mingling madly for the moment
    in cider-cup.
The ultimate alteration of the telegraph.

11.

The game is over ; yet for me never over :
For me it remains a memory and meaning wondrous
    mystical.

Bat-stroke and bird-voice (tally of my soul) "slog, slog, slog."

The jubilant cry from the flowering thorn to the flowerless willow, "smite, smite, smite."

(Flowerless willow no more—but every run a late-shed perfect bloom.)

The fierce chant of my demon brother issuing forth against the demon bowler, "hit him, hit him, hit him."

The thousand melodious cracks, delicious cracks, the responsive echoes of my comrades and the hundred thence-resulting runs, passionately yearned for, never, never again to be forgotten.

Overhead meanwhile the splendid silent sun, blending all, fusing all, bathing all in floods of soft ecstatic perspiration.

R.

"*BEHOLD! I AM NOT ONE THAT GOES TO LECTURES.*"

By W. W.

BEHOLD! I am not one that goes to Lectures or the
    pow-wow of Professors.
The elementary laws never apologise: neither do
    I apologise.
I find letters from the Dean dropt on my table—
    and every one is signed by the Dean's
    name—
And I leave them where they are; for I know
    that as long as I stay up
Others will punctually come for ever and ever.
    I am one who goes to the river,
    I sit in the boat and think of "life" and of
    "time."
How life is much, but time is more; and the
    beginning is everything,
    But the end is something.
I loll in the Parks, I go to the wicket, I swipe.
I see twenty-two young men from Foster's watching
    me, and the trousers of the twenty-two
    young men.
I see the Balliol men *en masse* watching me. The
    Hottentot that loves his mother, the untu-

tored Bedowee, the Cave-man that wears
only his certificate of baptism, and the Pata-
gonian that hangs his testamur with his
scalps.

I see the Don who ploughed me in Rudiments
watching me: and the wife of the Don
who ploughed me in Rudiments watching
me.

I see the rapport of the wicket-keeper and umpire.

I cannot see that I am out.

Oh! you Umpires!

I am not one who greatly cares for experience,
soap, bull-dogs, cautions, majorities or a
graduated Income-tax,

The certainty of space, punctuation, sexes, institu-
tions, copiousness, degrees, committees,
delicatesse, or the fetters of rhyme—

For none of these do I care: but least for the
fetters of rhyme.

Myself only I sing. Me Imperturbe! Me
Prononcé!

Me progressive and the depth of me progressive,

And the βάθος, *Anglicé* bathos

Of me chanting tó the Public the song of Simple
Enumeration.   Q.

BALLADE OF ANDREW LANG.

Answer, in form of Ballade, to a Freshman of Merton College.

You ask me, Fresher, who it is
　Who rhymes, researches, and reviews,
Who sometimes writes like Genesis,
　And sometimes for the Daily News:
　Who jests in words that angels use,
　　And is most solemn with most slang:
　Who's who—who's which—and which is whose?
　　Who can it be but Andrew Lang?

Quips, Quirks are his, and Quiddities,
　The epic and the teacup Muse,
Bookbindings, Aborigines,
　Ballades that banish all the Blues,
　Young Married Life among Yahoos,
　　An Iliad, an Orang-outang,
　Triolets, Totems, and Tattoos—
　　Who can it be but Andrew Lang?

Ah Ballade makers! tell me this,
　When did the hardest rhymes refuse
The guile that filled that book of his
　With multiplying Xs and IIs?
　You see me shuffle in his shoes,
　　You hear me stammer where he sang,
Who cannot charm you as I choose,
　　Who cannot be an Andrew Lang.

ENVOY.

Fresher! he dwelt with Torpid Crews,
　And once, like you, he knew the pang
Of Mods, of Greats, of Weekly Dues,
　And yet he is an Andrew Lang!

BALLAD OF THE UNIVERSITY JUBILEE ADDRESS, *June*, 1887.

To commemorate the story
Of fifty years of glory,
Which our nation in happiness had spent
A Deputation splendid,
And not to be transcended,
Was decreed at Convocation to be sent—to be sent.

There were Proctors in their ermine
(Which is torn from ribs of vermin),
And the purple pride of Provosts and of Pres.—
To advance in order flocking
(Pumps and tights and white silk stocking),
And present congratulation on their knees—on their
knees.

So with innocent elation
They got out at Windsor station,
Shyly crowded round their Chancellor like sheep;
Then gayer than a marriage,
Were all packed into a carriage,
On the top of one another in a heap—in a heap.

F

They were landed at the Palace,
Like the passengers from Calais,
On the steam-ships of Sir Edward Watkin, Bart.;
Then set down to recreation
At a sumptuous collation,
Till the Chamberlain said "Now's the time to start—
    time to start."

Then the Deputation found Her,
And the Life Guards all around Her,
With their brandished swords and uniforms of red;
And Her Majesty all gracious,
Likewise looking most sagacious,
With her sceptre and the crown upon her head—
    on her head.

Now the Chamberlain says "Steady!"
And all settle themselves ready,
With a look of joy and loyalty combined—
Save a Head who blushed and sidled,
For his armourer had idled,
So he'd had to leave his toasting-fork behind—fork
    behind.

And the Orator delivered
His Address, although he shivered,

(Being bolder at Encaenia than at Court);
    But Her Majesty just smiling,
    Said at once without beguiling,
"Very sorry I'm obliged to cut it short—cut it
    short."

    Then the Deputation tacking, ·
    To the door continued backing,
Whilst the Chamberlain assisted in the rear;
    Till the evanescent glimmer
    Of the Presence growing dimmer,
Slowly faded never more to reappear—reappear.

                  K.

ON POLITICAL JESTING.

Mr. Reid :—" *I have not much to say upon this matter. My learned friend presents it to your lordships as a piece of academic banter.*"

O YES, I was there when he said it,
   In his own unapproachable style :
And—I hope that my statement you'll credit—
   I do not remember a smile.
The papers I read the day after,
   Reporting the words that he spoke,
Had inserted assuredly "Laughter,"
   If he 'd meant the remark as a joke.

Was it all "in a spirit of banter,"—
   Not meant as a serious attack,—
When he said that a Parnellite ranter
   Was something like Whitechapel "Jack"?
When he hinted that Healy and Dillon,
   And similar pestilent folk,
Resembled a commonplace villain,
   Was he only intending a joke?

ON POLITICAL JESTING.

We thought his rhetorical vigour,
  His arguments' fervour and weight,
Recalled the majestical figure
  Of Cicero saving the State;
But the State must find others to save it,
  New champions the Cause must invoke;
For the speaker has made affidàvit
  That he only intended a joke.

Was it thus (we would ask him) that Tully,
  By Antonius or Catiline pressed,
Would have deigned his consistence to sully,
  Explaining he said it in jest?
Alas! for our phrases sonorous
  Are merely frivolity's cloak—
And Demosthenes' self would assure us
  That he meant the Philippics in joke!

A. G.

DULCE EST DESIPERE IN LOCO.

ITE, vos Oxonienses,
Et praesertim Mertonenses,
Bellicos stringatis enses!

Custos, Doctor, Magistratus,
Stat catenis oneratus,
In judicium sublatus.

"Vultu vir spectande tristi,
Ecquid culpae admisisti,
Aut injuriam fecisti?

"Nonne contra bonos mores
Tot Hibernos senatores
Nuncupasti *percussores*?

"An triumvirorum mentes
Sic exasperare tentes
Contra reos innocentes?

"Nisi culpa te purgabis,
Atque crimen expiabis,
Luculentam poenam dabis."

Saevis indejectus fatis
Notae vir urbanitatis
Dat responsum delegatis.

" Olim contionabundus,
Totus teres et rotundus,
Fio pueris jucundus.

" Illis operam impendo—
Exemplaribus monendo,
Vel jocis alliciendo.

" Testor, judices severi,
Verbis ioca immisceri—
Tantum licet confiteri.

" Sed subtilitas jocorum
Nunquam penetrat Scotorum
Cerebrum causidicorum."

Quaesitores colloquuntur—
Omnes curae diluuntur,
Risu tabulae solvuntur.

THE GREAT HOME RULE MEETIN'.

Dec. 1888.

O TIM, have ye heard of thim Saxons
   And their iligant meetin' last year,
Which they held to demolish the tyrint,
   Mr. Sidgwick himsilf in the cheer?
Och! the desolate counthry of Erin
   Shall smoile with a tear in each oy,
Now Professors have mounted the shamrock,
   And humbled the brutal Viceroy,
               Dear boy,
   I am thrimbling with proide and with joy.

'Twas own uncle he was to the tyrint
   That bathes in the gore of our hearts,
But the oylids of Oireland shall quiver
   With the sunshine of Liberty's darts:
For he opened the beautiful meetin',
   And expressed his Gladstonian regret
That our frind Thorold Rogers was absint,
   Southwark's Radical champion and pet;
               You bet,
   Ivry cheek with our cryin' was wet.

And the great Universithy Masther
  (Was it Jowett or Broight that I mane?)
Couldn't follow the soigh of his bosom,
  And pronounce for the Plan of Campaign.
For the base Saxon Government blàgyards,
  Of thrue feelin' they haven't a dthrop,
If he'd come with his badles and pokers,
  Bedad, they would shut up the shop,
                And lop,
  Or intoirely his salary stop.

Misther Freeman, ould Liberty's backbone,
  Said that none could call names like the boys,
'Twas the Oirish so nate were at toitles,
  And the rale indepindence and noise;
And 'twas *he* was the man to detarmine,
  And, faith, nivir fear but he would,
For each conthradictorin' scoundthrill
  He'd thrate as he thrated that rude
              Jim Froude;
  If he got, he could give back as good.

      *   *   *   *   * 1

[1] *A stanza is here advisedly omitted.*

Thin came Murray, John's College, the darlint!
An Austhralian from over the say.
May the Saints shower blissins upon him,
    And help him to get his degray!
May St. Pathrick put tips in his papers
    And cajole the Examiners tu!
May he grant him the fame of Mahaffy,
    And a leedy with ois of the blüe,
                His due,
    And to doy with the wealth of a Jew!

May the name of that jewel McGrigor
    Bring the blush to the forehead of slaves!
And may Heaven free Oireland for ivir
    From Saxons and Scotchmen and thaves!
Till the kings of our counthry returning
    Shall the Emerald island increase
With patates and whiskey and splindor,
    Now she's got on her side Misther Rhŷs;
                A pleece
In her heart he shall have without cease.

And the great Docthor Murray desarted
    His Scripthum the Land League to cheer,
Whose diction'ry like our own rints was
    Six pay-days or more in arrear:

And the Austrians, Rooshians, and Saxons,
  How he thrampled them into the dust,
And the tyrints all over the wide wurrld
  Who said if men promised, they must:
            Disgust
  Filled his soul till he couldn't but bust.

Then the editor well-known of Johnson
  (A divil who hated the Whigs),
And shure but I am Misther Parnill
  Denounced them himself, the mane pigs!—
Och! the darlint American Fanians,
  Across the Atlantical wave,
Will lift up their hands and their voices,
  Now that Oxford has larnt to be brave—
           God save
  The thrue boys that know how to behave!

                  LARRY O'TOOLE.

                      K.

FIRE!

By Sir W. S.

Written on the occasion of the visit of the United Fire Brigades to Oxford, May 1887.

I.

St. Giles's street is fair and wide,
  St. Giles's street is long;
But long or wide, may nought abide
  Therein of guile or wrong;
For through St. Giles's, to and fro,
The mild ecclesiastics go
  From prime to evensong.
It were a fearsome task, perdie!
To sin in such good company.

II.

Long had the slanting beam of day
Proclaimed the Thirtieth of May
Ere now, erect, its fiery heat
Illumined all that hallowed street,
And breathing benediction on
Thy serried battlements, St. John,

Suffused at once with equal glow
The cluster'd Archipelago,
The Art Professor's studio
  And Mr. Greenwood's shop ;
Thy building, Pusey, where below
The stout Salvation soldiers blow
  The cornet till they drop ;
Thine, Balliol, where we move, and oh !
  Thine, Randolph, where we stop.

III.

But what is this that frights the air,
And wakes the curate from his lair
  In Pusey's cool retreat,
To leave the feast, to climb the stair,
  And scan the startled street ?
As when perambulate the young
And call with unrelenting tongue
  On home, mamma and sire ;
Or voters shout with strength of lung
  For Hall & Co's Entire ;
Or sabbath-breakers scream and shout
The band of Booth, with drum devout,
Eliza on her Sunday out,
  Or Farmer with his choir :—

IV.

E'en so, with shriek of fife and drum
  And horrid clang of brass,
The Fire Brigades of England come
  And down St. Giles's pass.
Oh grand, methinks, in such array
To spend a Whitsun Holiday
  All soaking to the skin!
(Yet shoes and hose alike are stout;
The shoes to keep the water out,
  The hose to keep it in.)

V.

They came from Henley on the Thames,
  From Berwick on the Tweed,
And at the mercy of the flames
They left their children and their dames,
To come and play their little games
  On Morrell's dewy mead.
Yet feared they not with fire to play—
The pyrotechnics (so they say)
  Were very fine indeed.

ᛁ

VI.

(PS. BY L—D M——Y.)

Then let us bless Our Gracious Queen and eke
   the Fire Brigade,
And bless no less the horrid mess they've been and
   gone and made;
Remove the dirt they chose to squirt upon our best
   attire,
Bless all, but most the lucky chance that no one
   shouted "Fire!"

Q

AN OXFORD MARTYR:

An incident of the Donegal Campaign of April, 1889.

IT was two gallant Balliol men, that went across
  the sea;
It also was that statesman bold, O'C-nybeare, M.P.:
With grief and indignation the enormities they saw
Of the base and brutal Balfour, and the myrmidons
  of Law.

As they marked the destitution of the tenants of
  Gweedore,
Their political philanthropy inflamed them more
  and more:
And they felt an inward prompting to provide them
  bread and tea,
Did H-rrison, and B-nson, and O'C-nybeare, M.P.

"When tyrants put O'Brien in gaol, we smuggled
  meat and beer in,
And vindicated partially the liberties of Erin:

Although we cannot raise the siege, at least we'll
    feed the garrison."
(Thus spake the bold O'C-nybeare to B-nson and
    to H-rrison.)

"In England public feeling is for payment of a debt,
But England is behind the times in certain things
    as yet:
And the man's a mere oppressor, as I've said in
    Parliament,
Who would ask an Irish tenant for a portion of
    his rent.

"Then we'll feed these bold insolvents, as we fed
    O'Brien before,
And do in fair Falcarragh what we did at Tullamore!
The Secretary's myrmidons no terrors have for me:
For the Game of Law and Order's up," said
    C-nybeare, M.P.

They have purchased bread and butter, and also
    tea galore—
But windows had those tenants none, and dared
    not ope the door:

O then, my valiant H-rrison! none other 'twas
    than you
That took the victuals to the roof and passed them
    down the flue!

But 'twere better he'd been studying the history
    of Greece
Than evading the detection of a cordon of police:
It is safer reading "Contracts" on Isis' peaceful
    shore,
Than assisting their infringement by the tenants
    of Gweedore.

For the tyrant sent his minions with instructions
    for to catch
That gallant young philanthropist, descending from
    the thatch,
And posterity will shudder as it listens to the tale,
How a Balliol undergraduate was lodged in Derry
    gaol.

There is woe in Fisher's Buildings, and the Front
    Quad's wrapped in gloom,
And the bones of Dervorguilla are uneasy in the
    tomb:

While the Pr-sident of Tr-nity can't understand
    at all
Why he does not hear the organ and the banjo
    in the Hall.

Alas, heroic H-rrison! ochone and wirrasthrue!
Yet what you did for others, sure some will do
    for you :
And whiskey down the chimney of your cell, we'll
    hope, they'll pour,
To reward you for your services to freedom and
    Gweedore!

A. G.

UNITY PUT QUARTERLY[1].

By A. C. S.

THE Centuries kiss and commingle,
Cling, clasp and are knit in a chain;
No cycle but scorns to be single,
No two but demur to be twain,
'Till the land of the lute and the love-tale
Be bride of the boreal breast,
And the dawn with the darkness shall dovetail,
  The East with the West.

The desire of the grey for the dun nights
Is that of the dun for the grey;
The tales of the Thousand and One Nights
Touch lips with "The Times" of to-day.—
Come, chasten the cheap with the classic;
Choose, Churton, thy chair and thy class,
Mix, melt in the must that is Massic
  The beer that is Bass!

[1] *Suggested by an Article in the* Quarterly Review *enforcing the unity of literature ancient and modern, and the necessity of providing a new School of Literature in Oxford.*

Omnipotent age of the Aorist !
Infinity freely exact,—
As the fragrance of fiction is fairest
If frayed in the furnace of fact—
Though nine be the Muses in number
There is hope if the handbook be one,—
Dispelling the planets that cumber
 The path of the sun.

Though crimson thy hands and thy hood be
With the blood of a brother betrayed,
O Would-be-Professor of Would-be,
We call thee to bless and to aid.
Transmuted would travel with Er, see
The Land of the Rolling of Logs,
Charmed, chained to thy side, as to Circe
 The Ithacan hogs.

O bourne of the black and the godly !
O land where the good niggers go,
With the books that are borrowed of Bodley,
Old moons and our castaway clo' !
There, there, till the roses be ripened
Rebuke us, revile, and review,
Then take thee thine annual stipend
 So long over-due.
       Q.

TO X.

I WILL not mention, Love, thy name,
  Because I do not know it;
Nor could I hand it down to fame,
  Not being, Love, a poet.

I yearn, I languish more or less,
  Fritter away my life,
And yet I can't so much as guess
  Thy name, my future wife.

Sometimes I think I'll take to verse,—
  Professional ambition
Impels a lover to rehearse
  The woes of his condition;

But to depict an abstract love
  I fear is barely possible,
Since Bishop Berkeley seems to prove
  She's by no means cognoscible.

And soon as e'er I ask the Muse
  To help me to my aim,
She says her rule is to refuse
  Without the Lady's name.

Publish or not, it's all the same,
    What makes her so decide is
The giving of the fair one's name
    Is proof of *bona fides.*

Perhaps, Love, 'tis the same with you;
    You wonder oft and sigh
"Ah who is he will come to woo?"
    Be happy, Love, 'tis I.

Though Algebra I fairly hate
    And problems are vexations,
Let's try, Love, to express our state
    And solve it by equations.

Let x denote my future wife;
    Years 25 I've run;
If y be I, then when, my Life,
    Will $x + y$ be 1?

A plague on problems for a cheat,
    Such tasks were not for me meant,
Let's rather try, Love, when we meet,
    The Method of Agreement.
                    F. P. W.

THE GARDEN OF CRITICISM.

With humble apologies to " The Garden of Proserpine."

BLUNT beyond brute or Briton,
  Crowned with calm quills she stands,
Who gathers all things written
  With cold unwriting hands.
Her pampered praise is sweeter
Than friends' who fear to greet her,
To poetlings that meet her
  From many schools and lands.

She waits for each and other,
  She will not heed their prayer
That she was such another
  As those before her chair;
Dazed with dim dreams of dollars,
Masters and slaves and scholars,
With dank and dubious collars,
  And sad superfluous hair.

To each she giveth sentence,
  To some, perchance, rewards;
Or rules to ripe repentance
  With snows of stern regards.
Before her Fame sinks shaken—
Pale poets tempest-taken,
Sweet Shakespeare broiled to Bacon,
  Red strays of ruined bards.

She is not sure of gleaning
  By threat or call or curse
The curious crumbs of meaning
  That rugged rhymes may nurse.
Sighing that song should canker,
Her heart begins to hanker
For pages even blanker
  Than blank Byronic verse.

From too much love of Browning,
  From Tennyson she rose,
And sense in music drowning,
  In sound she seeks repose.
Yet joys sometimes to know it,
And is not slow to show it,
That even the heavenliest poet ·
  Sinks somewhere safe to prose.

Then rhyme shall rule o'er reason,
  And Swinburne over Time,
And panting poets seize on
  Each continent and clime ;
Aching alliteration,
Infantine indignation,
Eternal iteration
  Wrapt in eternal rhyme.

R. L. B.

TITANIA.

By Lord T———n.

So bluff Sir Leolin gave the bride away.
And when they married her, the little church
Had seldom seen a costlier ritual.
The coach and pair alone were two-pound-ten,
And two-pound-ten apiece the wedding-cakes ;—
Three wedding-cakes. A Cupid poised a-top
Of each hung shivering to the frosted loves
Of two fond cushats on a field of ice,
As who should say "*I* see you."—Such the joy
When English-hearted Edwin swore his faith
With Mariana of the Moated Grange.

For Edwin, plump head-waiter at The Cock,
Grown sick of custom, spoilt of plenitude,
Lacking the finer wit that saith, "I wait,
They come; and if I make them wait, they go,"
Fell in a jaundiced humour petulant-green,
Watched the dull clerk slow-rounding to his cheese,
Flicked a full dozen flies that flecked the pane—
All crystal-cheated of the fuller air,

Blurted a free "Good-day t'ye," left and right,
And shaped his gathering choler to this end :—

"Custom! And yet what profit of it all ?
The old order changeth giving place to new,
To me small change, and this the Counter-change
Of custom beating on the self-same bar—
Change out of chop. Ah me! the talk, the tip,
The would-be-evening should-be-mourning suit,
The forged solicitude for petty wants
More petty still than they,—all these I loathe
Learning they lie who feign that all things come
To him that waiteth. I have waited long,
And now I go, to mate me with a bride
Who is aweary waiting, even as I !"

But when the amorous moon of honeycomb
Was over, ere the matron-flower of Love—
Step-sister of To-morrow's marmalade—
Swooned scentless, Mariana found her lord
Did something jar the nicer feminine sense
With usage, being all too fine and large,
Instinct of warmth and colour, with a trick
Of blunting "Mariana's" keener edge
To "Mary Ann"—the same but not the same:
Whereat she girded, tore her crispéd hair,

Called him "Sir Churl," and ever calling "Churl!"
Drave him to Science, then to Alcohol,
To forge a thousand theories of the rocks,
Then somewhat else for thousands dewy-cool,
Wherewith he sought a more Pacific isle
And there found love, a darker love than her's.

Q.

CLEANSING FIRES.

FEB. 14TH, 1889.

You ask me, then, what caused the fire
    Which devastated Mansfield College—
What if I let the facts transpire
    Which lately came within my knowledge!
It was a piece of High Church guile
To wreck the Nonconformist pile.

From Pusey House at dead of night
    I heard the furtive clinking latch:
A bearded form stepped into sight
    With lantern dark and silent match;
Muttering some words about "her cup,"
And something like "her smoke went up."

From Keble's dark monastic cells
    I saw two men in surplice come:
One carrying explosive shells
    And one some crude petroleum.
" Down with it "—so I caught the sound—
" Down with it even to the ground ! "

And one came from S. Barnabas, †
  One from S. Philip and S. James ;
I heard them swearing " By the Mass "
  They would devote to vengeful flames
An Institution which was meant
To propagate unmixed Dissent.

And there is evidence which lends
  A tone of truth to the report,
That certain of a Bishop's friends
  Came slily from the Lambeth Court,
And laughed, and said they'd put to rights
Vex'd questions of "forbidden lights."

But why poor Fairbairn's house was fired
  While Hall and Library were spared
I have not hitherto inquired ;
  Yet some could tell us if they dared.
I think they might have burned at least
The Chapel for not facing East !

SIC PEDO CONTURBAT MATHO DEFICIT.

*Circiter hoc tempus, ut perhibent, vetus illud ac splendidissimum
Collegium di. Jo. Bapt. olim praediis, villis, agris ditissimum,
vel male rem procurando vel effusos adhibendo sumptus, adeo nihil
in loculis habebat ut neque Praesidenti neque Sociis quidquam nu-
merare posset : immo egestatis excusationem palam afferebat ne
quid pro rata parte in usus Academicos pendere cogeretur.*

PRAESIDENS, confectus annis,
Sedet vix opertus pannis
In Collegio Joannis.

Nam nec praedia vendendo
Nec impensas minuendo
Erit amplius solvendo.

Dicit "Agriculturalis
Nunc Depressio fit talis,
Ut conficiamur malis.

Summus inter Praesidentes,
Sociique esurientes,
Egestatem vix ferentes,

Quondam sole sub sereno
Qui gaudebant sinu pleno
Labant aere alieno."

Quid si jam suffragia dentur
Ne in posterum morentur
Aut fortasse excusentur

Contributiones istae
Universitatis cistae
E coll. divi Jo. Baptistae?

DAS KOCHMANNSLIED.

De inclined reader vill rememper dat de Gambridge shentleman men-
dioned in dis Lied vas write a book on de TIMAEUS *of Blado mit so*
moosh errordoms ge-filled dat der Logiksbrofessor Kochmann haf
mit anoder book ge-antworded. Mitvhiles haf he a vork ge-written
deaching how de philosopedevhcelsherumwirbelnde man shall de
hosdile cavallrie bevilderfy, ash in de hereafderfolgende pallad ish sed
oudt, und dere ish a bicture of him und his gomrades in DE ILLUSH-
DRADED LONTON NEWS, *to show dat de boet shpeaks de Troot.*

Id vas an audumn afdernoons, vay down in eighdy-
   nine,
De pully poys of Oxford vas geranked in pattle line,
All brebared for vight und ploonder, und 'tvas
   peautiful to see
De philosopede gontingent und de footman-cavallrie.

At Abenddämmerung a scoud coom hollering droo
   de camp,
"Rouse dere, rouse dere, Herr copitain, it's dime
   for us to tramp!
De repels ish at Culham, und ash far ash I
   couldt see
Dey's blayin' at lawn-tennis vhile dey trinks nach-
   mittag tea."

Ash vhen upon die Mitternacht, shouldt he a progdor
    meet,
Schnell scoots de cownless untergrat all down de
    hohe shtreet,
So flewed each pold Freiwillige. "Make all de
    shpeed you can,
Der Teufel put dese vellers droo !" so gried der
    Kochemann.

Den o'er de Mädel's Brücke die Soldaten reiten
    gehen
Py de allerverfluchte rifer und de allerverdammte
    plain ;
Und immer amit de vhirling vheels rote foremost
    in de van
Dot gyrotwistive Knasterbart, der edle Kochemann.

So hoory, hoory, on dey rote, philosópedes und all,
Dough de troompeter (vrom Merton) cot a most
    drementous fall,
Und de foot-cavallrie Hauptman saidt (like Sherman)
    priefly " D——n !"
Vhen he found his callant Kriegspferd reguisitioned
    for de dram.

H 2

Boot vhen de repel Reiterei coomed doondering on
    his droop
Mit efery brebaration um de Kochemann zu scoop,
He oop-ended his philosopede, und lyin' on de
    cround,
Like Toddie in de 'Merican book, shoost made de
    vheels go round.

Oop-ended too de repel's horse, und down de repel
    boomped,
Den on him shtraighd der Kochemann wie Doon-
    derblitz geshoomped,
Und ashked his brosdrade enemy ash o'er him he
    tid shtoop,
" Peliev'st dou in de Demiurge ? If so, I lets you
    oop."

"I don't know nix apout soosh dings, no more
    dan 'pout Home Rule,
You'd scarcely find a Cladstonite dot's ganz so crate
    a fool,
I'm greener ash a freshman, ash a shtatesman moosh
    more blind,
More ignorant ash de Gambridge men—for dey reads
    Archer Hind."

"Shtand oop, yoong man," der Kochmann gried,
    und blaced him on his feet,
"By vay of ransom you moost schvear my ladest
    vork to readt,
If *ve* ish daken brisoners, id dakes moosh geld to
    free us,
I *gifs* to you mein liddle book, dot treats of de
    Timaeus."

Wer kommt so lustig vhile de great Urbummellied
    he sings?
Dot ish der valiant Kochmann, und he smile like
    efery dings.
Who's dot ge-cooming afder him, mit soosh a gloomy
    look?
Dot's de oonhobby brisoner, who's cot to readt dot
    book!

                      S. T.

A LETTER.

Addressed during the Summer Term of 1888 *by* MR. ALGERNON
DEXTER, .*Scholar of* —— *College, Oxford, to his cousin,* MISS
KITTY TREMAYNE, *at* —— *Vicarage, Devonshire.*

DEAR KITTY,
  At length the Term's ending;
 I'm in for my Schools in a week;
And the time that at present I'm spending
 On you should be spent upon Greek:
But I'm fairly well read in my Plato,
 I'm thoroughly red in the eyes,
And I've almost forgotten the way to
 Be healthy and wealthy and wise.
So "the best of all ways"—why repeat you
 The verse at 2.30 a.m.,
When I'm stealing an hour to entreat you,
 Dear Kitty, to come to Commem.?

Oh come! You shall rustle in satin
 Through halls where Examiners trod:
Your laughter shall triumph o'er Latin
 In lecture-room, garden and quad.

They stand in the silent Sheldonian—
  Our orators, waiting—for you,
Their style guaranteed Ciceronian,
  Their subject—"the Ladies in Blue":
The Vice sits arrayed in his scarlet;
  He's pale, but they say, he dissem-
-bles by calling his Beadle a "varlet"
  Whenever he thinks of Commem.

There are dances, flirtations at Nuneham,
  Flower-shows, the procession of Eights:
There's a list stretching *usque ad Lunam*
  Of concerts and lunches and fêtes:
There's the Newdigate, all about 'Gordon,'
  —So sweet, and they say it will scan.
You shall flirt with a Proctor, a Warden
  Shall run for your shawl and your fan.
They are sportive as gods broken loose from
  Olympus, and yet very em-
-inent men. There are plenty to choose from,
  You'll find, if you come to Commem.

I know your excuses: Red Sorrel
  Has stumbled and broken her knees;
Aunt Phœbe thinks waltzing immoral;
  And "Algy, you are such a tease;

It's nonsense, of course, but she *is* strict";
 And little Dick Hodge has the croup;
And there's no one to visit your "district"
 Or make Mother Tettleby's soup.
Let them cease for a se'nnight to plague you;
 Oh leave them to manage *pro tem.*
With their croups and their soups and their ague,
 Dear Kitty, and come to Commem.

Don't tell me Papa has lumbago,
 That you haven't a frock fit to wear,
That the curate "has notions, and may go
 To lengths if there's nobody there,"
That the Squire has "said things" to the Vicar,
 And the Vicar "had words" with the Squire,
That the Organist's taken to liquor,
 And leaves you to manage the choir:
For Papa must be cured, and the curate
 Coerced, and your gown is a gem;
And the moral is—Don't be obdurate,
 Dear Kitty, but come to Commem.

"My gown? Though, no doubt, sir, you're clever
 You'd better leave such things alone.
Do you think that a frock lasts for ever?"
 Dear Kitty, I'll grant you have grown;

But I thought of my "scene" with McVittie
  That night when he trod on your train
At the Bachelor's Ball. "'Twas a pity,"
  You said, but I knew 'twas Champagne.
And your gown was enough to compel me
  To fall down and worship its hem—
(Are "hems" wearing? If not, you shall tell me
  What is, when you come to Commem.)

Have you thought, since that night, of the Grotto?
  Of the words whispered under the palms,
While the minutes flew by and forgot to
  Remind us of Aunt and her qualms?
Of the strains of the old *Journalisten*?
  Of the rose that I begged from your hair?
When you turned, and I saw something glisten—
  Dear Kitty, don't frown; it *was* there!
But that idiot Delane in the middle
  Bounced in with "Our dance, I—ahem!"
And—the rose you may find in my Liddell
  And Scott when you come to Commem.

Then Kitty, let "yes" be the answer.
  We'll dance at the 'Varsity Ball,
And the morning shall find you a dancer
  In Christ Church or Trinity hall.

And perhaps, when the elders are yawning,
 And rafters grow pale overhead
With the day, there shall come with its dawning
 Some thought of that sentence unsaid.
Be it this, be it that—" I forget," or
 " Was joking "—whatever the fem-
-inine fib, you'll have made me your debtor
 And come,—you *will* come? to Commem.

Q.

A REPLY

From Miss Kitty Tremayne *to* Mr. Algernon Dexter, *declining his invitation to the Encaenia of June* 1888, *on the ground that she proposes to attend the University Extension Summer Meeting in the Long Vacation of the same year.*

Dear Algy,
How could you suppose that
I care for your silly Commem.
Every Home Reading Circle well knows that
Such gaieties are not for them.
I am bent upon probing life's mystery,
And I write seven essays a week,
I read pure mathematics and history,
And high metaphysics and Greek.
I care not for balls and flirtations,
I am dull 'mid frivolity's throng,
But I pine for quadratic equations
In the studious repose of the Long.

I really don't know what you'll say to
The remarkable progress I've made :
Like you I can prattle of Plato,
Like you I can pilfer from Praed.

I have come to believe in the mission
　Of woman to civilise man;
To teach him to know his position,
　And to estimate hers—if he can.
Perhaps you would rather I'd greet you
　With snatches of music-hall song:
Ah, I fear I'm not likely to meet you
　In those serious hours of the Long.

You once said I danced like a fairy,
　Yet are dances but circles and squares,
And "quadrata rotundis mutare"—
　(It is Horace, dear Algy)—who cares?
Oh, if squaring the circle were possible!
　How I'd work to that end night and day.
Still, the Infinite *may* be cognoscible,
　And 'tis rapture to think that it may.
These, these are the thoughts that come o'er one;
　These high aspirations belong—
Not to luncheons and concerts that bore one,
　But—to serious life in the Long.

From lecture to lecture instructive
　I shall hurry with note-book and pen,
Mr. Harrison, preacher seductive,
　Will discourse upon eminent men;

Dr. Murray will tell how his Dictionary
  May inform generations to come ;
And a Bishop will talk about Fiction, ere I
  Return to my parish and home.
Yes, learning would cease to be labour,
  Though I studied the tongue of Hong Kong,
With a Dean or a Tutor for neighbour
  In my still College rooms in the Long.

I can gaze at the stars from your towers,
  Till the summer nights pale into dawns ;
I can wander with Readers in bowers,
  I can walk with Professors on lawns.
And oh, if from skies unpropitious
  Gentle rain in soft drizzle should fall,
There are chances of converse delicious,
  Tête-à-tête in the Cloister or Hall.
There's a feeling one has towards one's teacher—
  Dear Algy, don't say that it's wrong—
This communion of souls is a feature
  Of our shy student life in the Long.

You won't come. You'll be thinking of cricket,
  Or perhaps of lawn-tennis or sport,
You'll be studying the state of a wicket
  Or measuring the length of a court.

You'll be watching the stream and the weather,
  With your heart in your flies and your hooks;
You will tramp after grouse o'er the heather,
  While at Oxford I toil o'er my books.
So adieu: I've an essay just set me,
  And 'tis dinner time—there goes the gong;
And—dear Algy, you won't quite forget me,
  When I'm reading so hard in the Long?

X. Y. Z.

Mr. Algernon Dexter *appears to have been so much annoyed by the receipt of this letter as to forget alike his scholarship and his Praed, and to respond in the fresh and nervous vernacular of the Undergraduate of the period.*

DEAR KITTY,
  You used to be jolly,
 And I'd stand a good deal for your sake,
But, Great Scott! of all possible folly
  This last folly of yours takes the cake.
Why, you'd come up a mere carpet-bagger,
  And though Bishops and Dons boss the show,
And you think that it's awfully swagger,
  You would find that it's awfully slow.
Your friends say you're trying to rile 'em,
  And your enemies snigger and grin;
If they run you for Earlswood Asylum,
  By Jingo! you'd simply romp in.
You were always a bit of a dreamer,
  But you're coming it rather too strong,
And I'll write you a regular screamer
  If you dare to come up in the Long.
                              X. Y. Z.

OUR OWN NEWDIGATE:
BELISARIUS.

GREAT Belisarius, thy glorious name
Is half a synonym itself for Fame.
In the dark clouds she rears her lofty crest,
Eftsoons in solemn splendour sinks to rest:
So sinks the day-star in the Ocean bed
And yet anon repairs his drooping head
With the best colours that the sea affords,
And shines in splendour awful, O ye Gods!
  My hero was a Thracian by his birth,
A race as tough as any upon earth:
Born where the North wind, sweeping o'er the
    snows,
Straight from the chamber of the Ice King blows,
Rushes in whirlwinds up the mountain steeps,
Now howls in fierceness, now in sorrow weeps,
Then with a mighty gust essays to launch
Down the abyss the thundering avalanche,
Hurls the lithe wild goat screaming from the height,
Then drops his goat-herd spinning out of sight,
Drives the lush eagle from his fragrant lair,
Chills the wan seal or amorous polar bear:

Rude and relentless in its thrilling power,
Yet waits alike the inevitable hour,
For North-wind, hero, polar bear, or slave,
The paths of glory lead but to the grave.
   Then Belisarius left his Thracian home
To seek his fortune 'neath the star of Rome,
In the imperial guards he found a place,
Then sought and won, sweet boon, the imperial grace.
(This Emperor was Justinian of the Institutes,
Which part of our Oxford Law School up here
      constitutes.)
Like Paris handsome and like Hector brave,
His person stalwart and his manner· naive,
He was all round admittedly a hero
Whose rivals in comparison were zero.
Where Afric's sunny fountains roll their sand,
He came to war with his heroic band.
Skilled in the field his enemies to handle,
He made short work of the proverbial Vandal;
Cook'd for that horde their savage goose, and free
Sail'd homewards o'er the waters of the sea.
   His next exploits were in severe campaigns
Against the Goths upon the Italian plains.
Now all the Goths he fought were Arians
As well as most unnatural barbarians;

I

And so for Heaven he fought as well as for Justinian
In the extension of that great Emperor's dominion.
Ah! how shall scenes of war the care engage
Of peaceful poet in a peaceful age!
See at the walls of Rome the advancing host,
Rapine for watchword, Murder for their boast!
The red-mouthed Cannon and the Battering-ram,
The Arblast and the deadly Oriflamme,
All in the onset thunder their acclaim,
While charging savages advance amain.
Here the shields clash before the glittering lance,
There brigands with their bayonets advance:
Here Heroes calm, there Cowards lying low,
While cracks the rifle, twangs the unerring bow.
   Ingratitude, more strong than traitors' arms,
Effected more than savage war's alarms:
Like as the cloud the shepherd from afar sees
On the horizon rose the eunuch Narses,
Sad fruit of the imperial distrust,
As well as seed of mutual disgust;
Thus things were brought into a state precarious,
As well as most annoying to a proud man like
     Belisarius.
   As the rough ore by the refining art
Is purified to show the metal's heart,

With Belisarius the part of the refiner
Was played, we grieve to say, by Antonina.
No lustre's shed upon the hero's life
By his association with his wife.
Cheese has its maggots, and the rose its thorn,
Into this subject we need not be borne.
   Man is the sport of a superior Fate,
And princes' favour ends or soon or late.
He to whom no one else could hold a candle,
Conqueror of the Visigoth and Vandal,
In his old age, cast off, neglected, scorned,
By those whom his achievements had adorned,
Slunk through the streets, condemned, so it is said,
To look for eleemosynary aid,
Through rain or sunshine, hail or London fog
Attended only by his faithful dog.
Upon his breast he moves the thankless town
By "Blind but honest" on a placard shown.
Thus borne along through circumstances various
We end the history of Belisarius;
He left a name at which the world grew pale
To point a moral or adorn a tale.

                       K.

DISILLUSION.

THEY told me of the August calm
  Of Oxford in the Long Vacation,
How rarely plies th' infrequent tram
  'Twixt Cowley and the Railway Station;
How Undergraduates are gone
  Or peaks to climb or moors to shoot on,
And none remains but here a Don
  And there a speculative Teuton:

How in the Parks you seldom see
  The terminal perambulator;
How tradesmen close at half-past three,
  And silence broods o'er Alma Mater.
Ah me! 'twas all a baseless dream;
  One thing they quite forgot to mention—
The recently developed scheme
  Of University Extension.

They told me Oxford in the Long
  A place of solitude and peace is:
They told me so—they told me wrong;
For every train imports a throng
  Of sisters, cousins, aunts, and nieces,

Who crowd the streets, who storm the Schools,
  With love of lectures still unsated;
They're subject to no kind of rules,
  And can't be proctorised or gated.

'Neath auspices majestical,
  Their guide some Principal or.Warden,
From morn to eve they throng the Hall,
  And all day long they "do" the Garden.
Upon one's own peculiar haunts
  They rudely pry—O times, O manners!
They strum the Pirates of Penzance
  On Undergraduates' pianners.

The Bursar entertains about
  A score of feminine relations,
Whilst I invoke my absent scout,
  And hope in vain my humble rations.
If this be Oxford in the Vac.,
  When all her sons afar are scattered,
If this be peace,—then give me back
  The Torpid wine, the tea-tray battered!

                                    A. G.

THE EDITOR'S FAREWELL.

FAREWELL to the labours of copy and proof,
    And the strain of redacting reviews,
And welcome a season of standing aloof
    From supplying a gap in the news!

Farewell to the toil of inventing remarks,
    Whether soothing, offensive or free;
So rest in the shade of thy vineyards, O Parks,
    No more to be troubled by me!

Hebdomadal Council, doomed never to rest,
    In withstanding the course of the Sun!
No more shall I scan your preambles with zest—
    For my race of existence is run.

Farewell, propagandists of Specialist Schools,
    Who scorn to provide for the mass;
Professors, farewell, who think Tutors are fools,
    And who moan (but don't wish) for a class!

Farewell, O Museum, too apt to prepare
  For success in supplying your wants,
By grasping a more than legitimate share
  And demanding inordinate grants!

Farewell to the poets, whose metrical skill
  Is hampered by weakness of rhyme!
Continue your sonnets and odes to distil,
  Fame is only a question of time.

Farewell, you deep thinkers, whose words should
    ensure
  A result of importance immense,
But remember in future, expressions obscure
  Are apt to throw doubt on the sense!

Farewell to each rival political scheme,
  Whether Patriot, Tory or Rad,
As well as to each philanthropical dream,
  Spook, Buddhist or Socialist fad!

Farewell to Athletics, whose writers forget,
  (Being chafed by grammatical curb,)
Their critical strictures in concords to set,
  Or the subject provide with its verb!

Farewell, O ye beautiful groves of the Press,
  Sweet haunt of the bulbul and dove,
Where the spirit of Learning was present to bless
  And the Muse ever hovered above!

Farewell to my critics, farewell to my foes,
  Farewell to each lover and friend!
The curtain has dropt on an editor's woes,
  For the editor's come to an end.

PROSE PIECES

TRANSLATION OF AN ARISTOTELIAN
FRAGMENT IN THE BODLEIAN.

CONCERNING Golf, and how many parts of it there
are, and how we ought to play it, and as many things
as belong to the same method, let us speak, beginning
from the Tee according to the nature of the treatise.
For there are some who begin not only after teeing
the ball, but also immediately after breakfasting
themselves: but this is not Golf, but incontinence or
even licentiousness. *Head of horses, + ...*

Now it is possible to play in several ways: for
perhaps they strike indeed, yet not as is necessary,
nor where, nor when; as the man who played in the
Parks and wounded the infant: for this was good for
him, yet not absolutely, nor for the infant. Where-
fore here as in other things we should aim at the
mean between excess and defect. For the player in
excess hits the ball too often, as they do at cricket;
and the deficient man cannot hit it at all, except by
accident (κατὰ συμβεβηκός): as it is related of the man
who kicked his caddie, as they do at football. For
the beginning is to hit it: and the virtue of a good

golfer is to hit well and according to reason and as the professional would hit. And to speak briefly, to play Golf is either the part of a man of genius or a madman, as has been said in the *Poetics*.

And because it is better to hit few times than many —for the good is finite, but the man who goes round in three hundred strokes stretches out in the direction of the infinite—some have said that here too we ought to remember the saying of Hesiod, "The half is better than the whole," thinking not rightly, according at least to my opinion: for in relation to your adversary it is much better to win the Hole than the Half. And Homer is a good master both in other respects and also here: for he alone has taught us how to lie as is necessary, both as to the hole (καθόλου), and otherwise.

Again, every art and every method, and likewise every action and intention aims at the good. Some, therefore, making a syllogism, aim at a Professor: for Professors, they say, are good (because dry things are good for men, as has been said in the *Ethics*), and this is a Professor: but perhaps they make a wrong use of the major premise. At any rate, having hit him, it is better to act in some such way as this, not as tragedians seek a recognition (ἀναγνώρισις); for this is most unpleasant (μιαρόν), and perhaps leads to a catastrophe. It is doubted, whether the man who killed his tutor with a golf-ball acted voluntarily or involuntarily; for on the one hand he did not do it deliberately, since no one deliberates about the results of chance, as, for instance, whether one will hit the ball this time at any rate or not: yet he wished to kill him, and was glad having done it: and probably on the whole it was a mixed action.

Are we, then, to call no man happy till he has finished his round, and, according to Solon, to look to the end? for it is possible to be fortunate for a long time and yet at last to fall into a ditch: and to the man in the ditch there seems to be no good any more, nor evil. But this is perhaps of another consideration: and, at any rate, it has been discussed sufficiently among the topics of swearing. But it is a question whether a caddie can be called happy, and most probably he cannot; those who seem to be so are congratulated on account of their hope (διὰ τὴν ἐλπίδα μακαρίζονται).

A. G.

HOW THUCYDIDES WENT TO THE TRIALS.

I. Now, in the end of this year, when Bellamaeus had three years of his archonship to run at Oxford, and in the middle of winter, when the collections-harvest was just in its prime, with which I have both been myself afflicted and have seen others suffering, there happened to be the great festival of Heracles Phileretmos.

II. Now, to the place where they row it may be travelled by the sacred wagons of Hephaestus, if the wind always blow steadily behind their sterns, in about half a day, and by a scratch octoreme or by a man of decent waist, marching on foot, in something less, so that as well on this account fewer men use the sacred wagons, and also because not only among the priests but especially the menials of Hephaestus, the custom is established rather to receive than to give, and it is more shameful in their eyes not to give, having been asked, than, having asked, not to obtain, notwithstanding which it seemed good to Thucydides, who wrote this history, an oof-ship from the Thraceward parts having lately come in, both otherwise to blow the expense and above all, having previously hired a crawler, not to spare the necessary sacrifice to the God, by whose conveyance when he had gone, himself the fourth, about the time of the full moon, to Moulsford, they marched at most seven stades into the inner country and piled arms at the temple of Dionysus used by the indigenous tribes of that coast.

III. And at this point they found those from the city in a state of sedition and gathered into knots, and evidently terrified by the mightiness of the stream; for the river Isis, flowing down from the mountains of Cotswold, through the land of the Godstovians and Eynshamites and the plain of Wytham, and having made an inundation, it both flooded part of the country, so that what was towpath is now peasoup, and suggested as a just conclusion that it would destroy any who did not anticipate it by scooting to the higher ground. So straightway they fell into the factions of the Parali, the Diacrii, and the Pedieis, whereof the Diacrii retired to the top of a hill that happened to be about, if in any way they might see the race, while the Parali tore along the towpath, running the risk with their bodies, but the Pedicis, being for the most part funks and . . .

(Hiatus in MS. valde deflendus.)

Of these factions, then, Thucydides joined the Parali, at once wishing to make a display of valour to obliterate the fiasco at Amphipolis, and considering his life and his exhibition alike ephemeral he thought it would be not idiotic, reaping his enjoyments speedily, to abandon the one, painlessly at the zenith of an anaesthetic excitement, rather than, surviving, to lose the other, shamefully, something having happened at Mods. And when the antagonistic octoremes appeared, it seemed to those looking on to be more like a solemn procession of some god, or a burying of those fallen in war, than a race: but straightway there was a clamour: but to Thucydides it seemed most according to custom to yell "Well rowed, Four!" since he also was a citizen of my own city: which I did, adding to it with an oath, reasonably, the mud simultaneously getting into my eyes and ascending my nose.

IV. Now there is a sacred ship, the Paralus, in which the high-priest [having previously taught the aspirants to practise all the gymnastic virtues in a small bireme of burden, built like a horse-transport] himself follows, uttering the needful curses and general truculence, by means of which he is most persuasive with the performers, and ragging the

pilots if anywhere he see them meditating the diek-
plus or other manœuvres which, while in war most
effective, entail an universal obloquy by their use in
a devotional exercise. But, when the race was over,
those on board the Paralus beached their vessel and
seemed likely, making a disembarkation, to invade
the country of the Parali. But they, anticipating
them, and shouting that the Parali were the right
possessors of the Paralus, that they were jiggered
if they'd walk back, and other expressions such as
nautical multitudes love to use, not only came to the
rescue but even boarded the ship, first chucking
their hats and sticks into the space forward of the
boiler, that there might be no repentance. But
Thucydides (deeming it monstrous if Tims should
chop off his hand like that of Aminias the brother of
the poet Aeschylus in the Persian business), holding
fast to his umbrella waved it in a circle, at the same
time exhorting others to go first, and calling the
local deities to witness that Tims was acting unjustly
in invading the land, and testifying that, if any
of the enemy suffer anything incurable from the
gamp, Thucydides is blameless.

V. But at length, a treaty having been made, the
original crew of the Paralus manifestly showed them-

selves to be horse-marines, being unable to push off from the land, where she was fast grounded. But at this juncture the Parali seized long poles and, encouraged by the opinion that two Parali are as good as about six horse-marines, shoving her off worked out their passage. And when he had just put out to sea, I espied the scribe, or second priest, of the rival cult of Heracles at Cambridge, who was a prisoner but not bound, nor did I see our own high-priest attempt anything revolutionary against him, as one who had contributed not a little to lick us in the preceding spring.

VI. And at the end of the same season, and on the same day as the naval show, the Temple of Dionysus and Aphrodite in the High[1] was partly burnt, although the worshippers had gone down the same day ; so that it was probably set alight by some one of those in power falling asleep on his candlestick. And the season ended, and the second year of the four, during which Thucydides read history.

C. E. M.

---

[1] *It will be remembered that Queen's College was partly burnt, as Thucydides states, on the last Saturday of Michaelmas Term, 1886. Herodotus considers the fire an act of felicitous arson by the God of Marriage, designed as a nuptial housewarming for the Provost. The ultra-rationalists at the time traced it* (putidius) *to a small fire in the Bursary, used for cooking the accounts.*

. . . . CERTAINLY there be some that delight in nakedness, and count it better to worship in great boots and a long cloke than in the richest apparel. I knew a nobleman of the West of England which made a wager in a waggishness that he would keep a chapel in a surplice and shoes, or as Livy hath it of the captives—

Ternis tantum vestimentis.

For which humour he was sent down. I hold it better that the college be answered some small matter for each garment that is wanting.

For freshers, I mislike not that they be asked to lunch, but it is a shameful and unblessed thing to give much hock to them that row. Also let coaches give many easies. I have known a fresher do two journeys to Iffley without queeching, when he was so raw as he would fain be standing up all the rest of the day. But these be toys.

A Head had need be wary how he admit black men. I hold it safest that they be ploughed in

K 2

Matric. For so shall the conceit of their own knowledge be beaten down in them, and they shall be less
likely to make war on the Vice-Chancellor. There
was in my time a Persian at Skimmery who conse-
crated his scout to be his priest, whereby the man
was cashiered, and his family miserably destituted.

Tacitus saith of a scout—

     Vestimenta et offas tanquam indagine capi.

I hold it not well that the scouts lurch all the gains.
To extinguish their peculations utterly is but a
bravery and a dreaming. But for the college to
connive at them, taking privily some part of the
spoils, commonly giveth best way; for so shall it
have them obnoxious and officious towards itself, and
the commoners shall learn that pleasure hath its
cost.   .

For divers instruments of music, surely it is a hard
thing to keep them all down to strait limits of time.
Let some difference be made. For the banjo, I
would have it free always, seeing it is the same as
the lyre of the ancients. I mislike the bones.. . . . .

*Here the MS. becomes illegible. Certain critics have objected
that Bacon was not a member of the University of Oxford, but of
Cambridge. Surely the merest schoolboy should know that Bacon
was for two years a resident at Teddy Hall, and that he was sent down*

A.D. 1572, *as there seemed no chance of his learning enough Greek to get through Smalls, although he had most of Abbott and Mansfield's Accidence copied out on his shirtsleeves. It is certain that he believed himself innocent* in his heart *and only wished thereby to benefit mankind. His words on the subject are:* " *I was the justest man that went in for Smalls these fifty years, but it was the justest plough done in the Schools these two hundred years.*"

C. E. M.

OF MUSICK.

It was truly devised of David, himself the greatest harper—

I am become a reproach among all mine enemies, but especially among my neighbours.

And Cosmus Duke of Florence had a desperate saying against them that play scales. "You shall see," saith he, "that we are bidden to forgive our enemies, but we are nowhere forbidden to make hay with the pianos of our friends." And certainly the nature of a musical man hath some composition of a smug. For them that play the cornet, it is right earth. The poet hath it better:

> Tuba, mirum spargens sonum,
> Scalas implet regionum,
> O, quâ musicâ tironum.

Macchiavel well noteth that if a man do play out of tune, he doth in some sort give a passport to faith: for so shall he bring in a new *primum mobile* that ravisheth all the music of the spheres. For smoking concerts, they are not amiss. Only let the songs be

not hearse-like airs, touching rooks or the rawness of *Ballrd or*
them that row. And it were well that the hall or
refectory wherein you sing be double-windowed, so
as the followers of Momus, which be many, have no
provand of invective. You shall see that in these days
there hath arisen a sect of zealants which make
psalmody in St. Giles so devoutly as putteth them of
Balliol out of office. Nay, they say that even hath a
negro of that college been so depraved by this over-
heat of zeal as he hath sat in the chair of scorners,
by a great revulsion of spirits, and goeth to roll-call.

Tantum religio potuit suadere malorum.

There be two swords against fiddlers, whereof the
first, which is to break their bones, would be kept in
seasonable use; the second, to break their fiddles, if
there be no remedy. But let this last be used in
closeness and secrecy, inasmuch as it will scarcely
be brooked that a man do deal so austerely in a kind
of civil judgment on his even clay. I have known a
fiddler, thus destituted of his toy, to fall into so fixed
a melancholy as he presently went off the hooks.
And to make this kind wholly desist, while the breath
is yet in them, is a bravery of the Stoics. So as that
opinion may be sent to Utopia.

But to speak in a mean.   That will not be amiss if a man so frame his actions as he may show that he liketh not this shindy, as by casting of small stones at windows whence sound of exercises doth proceed, or by speech of touch on occasion, as :—" You are a smug," " When did you leave off beating your grand-mother?" with many civil bullets in this sort, which shall do hurt to no man, but rather much good.   For Consalvo rightly noteth that you shall rarely see a musical man ready and prest for a quarrel, being themselves more full of jingles and sickly phantasms of the imagination, which cloud the spirits and check with a warlike composition.

Ovid saith of a company of flute-players : —

> Tibiaque effundit socialia carmina vobis
> At mihi funerea flebiliora tuba.

And that renowned prince, Sultan Mustapha, is said to have instituted a law that none should touch a flute, or as the Turk hath it with some crassness " spit-whistle," before he hath learned to play the same.

To speak now of the reformation and reiglement of music : the way would be briefly thus :—let a man that playeth classical music be gated, or, if he abate not, sent down.   For that, is a vein that would be bridled. Music for dancing is a thing of great state and pleasure, and herein would polkas be encouraged. And also it would not be misliked that those in great place, Vice-Chancellors, butlers, and the like, should sing nigger songs. For you shall see how prest they are to admit niggers to the foundations which they govern.

They say there hath been seen in the Low Countries a Head of a College which admitted men of war, of a fierce and turbulent temper, to play the music of their calling in the quad. This thing would not be imitated. For how shall the martial brayings of them that earn their bread

In cruore corporis alieni

sort well to the retired pensiveness of applied studies? But as Heads are commonly but like the thorn or briar which do wrong because they can do no other, so a man were best set up his rest at the last upon the hope of some posterior . . .

CAETERA DESUNT.

C. E. M.

FRAGMENTUM.

..... Isdem ferme diebus orta seditio Wiccamicos
concussit, quanto plures erant, tanto violentius. Ope-
rae pretium fuerit initia et causas eius rei breviter
expedire. erat inter Wiccamicos Julius Undergra-
duatus, procax moribus, non absurdus ingenio : hunc
Titus Cochlearius antiquae sanctitatis apud consules
reum postulaverat, tamquam famoso libello inlustres
feminas laesisset, ira an improbitate dubium. atque
ille in senatu exitiabiles Academiae feminas conques-
tus contumeliam tamen cum nequiret infitiari damna-
tur : de modo poenae multum ac diu agitatum, cum
alii in insulam deportandum alii virgis et more maio-
rum caedendum varie dissererent. vicere qui exsilium in praesens censerent : itaque statim urbe
excedere iubetur. additur custos abeunti Higgsius
Jimmius vetus aurigandi, qui usque ad primum lapi-
dem deduceret : et fuere inter plebem qui in via
interficere iussum dictitarent.

Namque vulgus Wiccamicorum iamdudum fremebat
et alienum casum propria ira indignabatur. igitur

exeuntem curia Undergraduatum circumstare, pren-
sare manus, suprema oscula petere : insontem culpae
clamitare, et ne sontem quidem damnandum. mox
ad portam flentes et vociferantes prosequuntur;
Higgsium cum reda opperientem minis et pugnis
proturbant, donec fessus pavidusque in tabernam
confugeret : inde solutis equis et abactis ipsi colla
iugo supponere, sibi placentes, ceteris ridiculi. nec
deerat ipse, quem trahebant, minitari patribus, Vice-
cancellarium ultorem poenae testari. sic ex urbe
deducitur.

Mox in domos reversis vastum primo silentium.
inclusi et maerentes cibi quoque et religionum usum
aversari: namque epulas solito lautiores patres populo
poni iusserant, levamentum doloris in praesens, in
posterum ultionem. sed illi prae ira famem pati
maluere;· horrendas illas epulas: invisa deorum
sacra. ubi priscam libertatem typorum? proinde
aliis quoque id exsilium exspectandum, si Professo-
rem verbo laederet, si Tutorem quamvis vero crimine
lacesseret. deinde in querelas et clamorem erum-
punt, alii Collectiones et atroces notas, alii Aristotelis
Ethica (Graecum librum) propriis nominibus incu-
santes : et adventanti nocte incendium etiam parant,
indignum facinus sed his moribus haud inusitatum.

neque interventu decani (publici servi id vocabulum)
mitigati ipsum ultro flammis imponebant, nisi missae
a procuratoribus litterae augescentem seditionem
paulatim compescuissent.   A. G.

WICCAMICOS] *Rei per se satis planae scriptor notae obscuritatis
aliquantum caliginis offudit. Caput autem Collegii cujusdam ita
mihi ambages percontanti (qua est Latinitate) explicat: " Auctori-
tates Novi Collegii hominem demiserunt quia fuisset editor scandalosi
periodicalis." Quo nihil facilius intellectu.*

THE DESTRUCTION OF DIDCOT.

' . . . Not long after these events the Temple of
Hephaestus at Didcot was burnt to the ground for
the first time, being built almost entirely of wood.
Of the origin of this fire I am unable to give any
certain account; but all may believe as they choose.
For the servants of the temple assert that it caught
fire of its own accord, saying in my opinion the thing
which is not, whereas the directors or high priests
say it was done by some sparks from the neighbouring city of Oxford. These things therefore are
so: but of the temple itself I think it right to give
a fuller account, both because it is notable on many
accounts, and chiefly for this. A sophist from Oxford may always be seen there: I know the man, but
I will not tell his name, and the reasons for which
he comes it is not lawful for me to mention. Also,
the temple has a covered way, in which there is
always the smell of an elephant. For this, although
I have enquired, I am unable to account, inasmuch
as I have never seen an elephant there myself, nor

have heard of it from any eye-witness. Indeed, it appears incredible that an elephant, being so huge a beast, could have entered a way so narrow: or if one entered at any time, he must have been much smaller than the elephants known to us. Let this, then, remain unknown; but the servants of the temple affirm that twice in every day a Dutchman enters the temple at a great speed in both directions. This I do not believe, for in addition they say that this Dutchman flies, whence "the flying Dutchman" has passed into a proverb among the inhabitants of Didcot. But how could a Dutchman, being of such a shape, fly? Also they make mention of a Zulu: but these tales I pass over, for the servants do not seem to speak the truth. And the reason is this. They wear garments of a green colour, emitting a powerful odour, which, when they have put them on, so intoxicates the brain that often they stand ringing a bell and beckoning the pilgrims to the wrong side of the temple, whereby many annually are slain, and many more go to places whither it is not meet for them to go. In this way I myself have come within sight of Didcot thrice on three successive days. And even if one should disbelieve, and act upon his own suggestion, he may yet chance to go wrong:

for they do not always lie. Otherwise prevision
would be easy. Now the carriages that convey
pilgrims are called in their language "trains," and
the road they call a "line." When the temple was
burnt, they say that a certain man called Gooch
rebuilt it in the following manner. As many trains
as came he diverted on to a side line, having made
one for the purpose, and there kept them until the
temple was finished, after which he again let them
all loose into the "station," as some call the temple.
I examined the skulls of those that died upon this
occasion, being chiefly the skulls of Oxonici, and
found them much smaller than is usual. Now of the
food of the inhabitants of Didcot, I can speak with
assurance, having myself tasted it. It consists chiefly
of cakes, which they prepare as follows . . . . Having
thus prepared them, they keep them for a space of
three years, during which it is death to eat one, and
even afterwards not without danger. These cakes
they dedicate to the Lady of Banbury, of whom the
following account is given. Having rings upon her
fingers, and some say even bells upon her toes, she
once rode into Oxford and there founded a college,
called Balliol College. The poet Bossades even
narrates that the horse wore a scholar's gown or

tunic on this occasion.   This I do not believe, but I am certain that she went : for another poet says with regard to her, " she shall have music wherever she goes," and there is much music in Balliol College. Now why there should be so much music I do not know, nor has any man been able to explain to me. But of this subject I have already treated in my published works.

Q.

THE NEW DON QUIXOTE.

Wherein is related the terrific adventure of the galley slaves, otherwise known as the adventure of the enchanted barque.

THE ingenious Cid Hamet Benengeli relates that after the adventure above set down, Don Quixote raised his eyes and saw coming up the river at a briskish pace a galley manned by eight rowers, all bound to the work with tight leathern fetters on their feet, and pounding away at their oars with the vigour suggested by despair and terror. With them there also came one man on horseback and three on foot; the cavalier, who wore a blood-coloured jerkin, was of a truculent aspect, and perpetually let fly at the captives in the boat with maledictions and scurvy taunts, while the infantry, fine personable varlets of some 13 stone, kept pace with the aforesaid cavalier in upbraiding the unhappy galley-slaves with their sloth, and browbeating them into mending their sorry progress.

When our knight had considered sufficiently the thin and miserable raiment of the prisoners and the arrogant bearing of those that had them in charge, he turned to Sancho and said, " Doubt not, Sancho, that in yonder knight you see the gigantic Gilberto-burno, famous not only as one of the most celebrated Stinks Dons in Spain, but also as a slashing and sagacious dialectician, who, merely in two epistles, overthrew the reactionary historian Fletchero of the Changed Visnomy, who had presumed to discuss with him polemically the Posterior Analytics of our common anatomy, and the discipline most fit to inflict on backsliding galley-slaves the maximum of torment and exertion. Unless indeed this be an enchanted barque of the sage Merlin, or the malig-nant magician Frisbon be here carrying off for his seraglio a bevy of captive princesses, transmogrified by his hellish arts into the seeming of squalid criminals."

And, having said so much, and commended him-self to his divine Dulcinea, without further parley he couched his lance, dug his spurs into Rozinante's spare ribs, and bore down on the poor "coach," for such it was, fully set on letting daylight through his carcase without more ado, and crying loudly :—" De-fend thyself, miserable monster, or instantly restore to freedom and liberty of thine own accord those whom thou holdest in durance in yonder enchanted barge."

The learned Cid here indulges in a sapient specu-lation on the probable issue of a tourney between two such champions, for the coach was a man of the first mettle, and one, as the saying is, not to be drubbed for a mere song, so that doubtless the passage of arms would have ended in one of the principals being cleft like a pomegranate, but, unhappily for the polite chroniclers of chivalry, he was mounted on a charger who joined the physique of Rozinante to the pacific and dilettante-like temper of one who draws a cab six days out of seven, and no sooner did he catch a hint of hostilities, than he instantly shook his ill-hung bones together and scoured across the plain more nimbly than a gazelle, and with the lungs of a dromedary.

Don Quixote, exulting in this tergiversation, commanded the galley to approach, and asked one of the crew for what offence he was now in such sorry case, and rated so soundly by yonder recreant knight.

He answered, "that it was for being heavy with his hands."

"For that only!" replied Don Quixote, "why,

I have heard say your light-fingered gentry are the more sinners. And you, sir ?"

This criminal, who was stroke, answered, "that he was abused for hurrying his own swing and so causing the rest to hang."

"Nay, friend," said Don Quixote, "surely thy logic is at fault, for in our province they say 'Let ropes race to hang a knave,' and, besides, the better speed thou makest to thine own justification by the grace of hemp, the sooner wilt thou remove thine evil example from the path of thy fellows. Nor, indeed, dost thou deserve, for merely exercising the office of tempter, to row in these craft, inasmuch as the office is a very ancient and necessary one, and, as the saying is, the broad road must have keepers to open its turnpikes as well as another."

He then asked the same question of the third, who made no reply, so downcast and melancholy was he; but the rest answered for him "that he was thus abused for a slow recovery, and, although their custodian had sworn his bellyful at him, he was still as far from being cured as ever."

"What !" said Don Quixote, "cure the sick with hard labour, and make them sound the sooner with scurvy jeers and curses !"

In this way Don Quixote examined each of the crew as to his offences, and found in no case any graver guilt than the apparently venial peccadilloes of hurrying or being slow, stiffening the hands or shrugging the shoulders, all of which appeared to our Manchegan to be, at the worst, merely solecisms against good breeding, or some trivial neglect of one's own convenience, or else personal misfortunes to be pitied rather than censured, and in every case quite out of measure with the barbarous enormity of the penalty. On which, turning to the whole string of them, he said, "From all you have told me, dear brethren, I make out that your punishments, at any rate, do not give you much pleasure; and that, perhaps, this one's want of nimbleness, another's despair of escaping justice, the feeble health of the third, and, lastly, the perverted judgment of your oppressor, may have been the causes of your failure and present sufferings, and it seems to me a hard case to make slaves of those whom Nature has made free. Moreover, sirs of the towpath," added Don Quixote, turning to the three pedestrians, "these poor fellows have done nothing to you; let each answer for his own sins yonder; Heaven will not forget to punish the wicked, or reward the good.

Finally, I desire, and it is my good pleasure, that laden with those straps which I have taken off your feet, and each carrying his oar, ye at once set out and proceed to the city of El Toboso, and there present yourselves before the lady Dulcinea del Toboso, and say to her that her knight sends to commend himself to her, and that ye recount to her in full detail all the particulars of this notable adventure, up to the recovery of your longed-for liberty ; and, this done, ye may go where ye will, and good fortune attend you."

The precise Cid Hamet is so curious as to recount that during this passage of arms, and the knight's discourse, Rozinante was busy with a light intrigue in a neighbouring pasture, that Dapple and Sancho surveyed the adventure with great sagacity and mutual understanding, Sancho reflecting that doubtless his master would be in the right to trounce the burly fellow for rating honest folk that were like to be Pope as soon as he, and that in the end Don Quixote remounted, and slowly walked Rozinante in the direction of the desert sierras of Cumnor, where he passed the night refreshing his soul with the lively image of his divine Dulcinea.

C. E. M.

AGYMNASTICUS; OR, THE ART OF
BOWLING.

PERSONS OF THE DIALOGUE.

SOCRATES, *who is the narrator.*
AGYMNASTICUS, *a reading man.*
ATHLETES, *a sportsman.*
And others who are mute characters.

I WENT the other day to witness the great gymnastic contest between eleven of our young men and the famous colonists, which was being celebrated in a field just outside the city. My only companion was Agymnasticus, whom I had induced, with great difficulty, to leave his books, for, as he explained to me, the time was close at hand when his learning was to be put to a very severe test, and he had therefore very little leisure. We got a good position, just on the edge of the enclosure, and we were lucky enough to find my friend Athletes standing near us. He was looking very excited, and, as I thought, somewhat sadder than usual. Well, Athletes, I said, how is the game going?

Very badly, said he, with a sigh; for, though the

colonists did badly, our men are doing much worse; four of our best wickets are down already for but two runs.

And why is this? I inquired.

.*J. R.*

That tall thin man there, whom they call the Daemon, is too much for them; it is he who has taken all the wickets. See, there goes another, he cried; that stout man who is now walking away is himself the fifth who has fallen, and the score is not yet ten.

It seems to me only natural, said I, that in such a contest as this the lean and wiry hound should prevail over the fat and clumsy. Truly, this Daemon must be a great batsman.

My dear Socrates, said he sharply, what are you saying? You betray an extraordinary ignorance of the game.

Then I am glad to have you at hand to correct me, I said; perhaps I should learn most quickly if you would answer a few questions which I should like to put to you about the game. You would admit, I suppose, that there is an art of bowling?

But he would not answer my question. I know nothing about art, he said; but I know exactly what you are after, Socrates; and I shall not answer you. And, disregarding me altogether, he turned to watch

the contest. I addressed myself therefore to Agymnasticus—What do you say, my friend? I asked;
is bowling an art or not?

Undoubtedly it is an art, he replied.

Very well, I said; let us then consider it with
reference to the other arts. In boxing, for instance,
is not he who is most expert in dealing blows, also
expert in parrying blows?

Very true, he said.

Again, in medicine, he who can produce a disease
is also best able to prevent one?

Certainly.

And he is the best guard of a military position who
is best able to take it?

Quite so.

Speaking generally, then, for I need not examine
all the arts separately, he who is best able to take
anything is also best at guarding, protecting, or
keeping it?

He is.

But the best bowler is best at taking wickets, is
he not?

Of course.

He is therefore best able to guard, keep, or protect
them?

True.

But is not he who is best able to guard or protect the wickets the best batsman?

Yes.

It seems, therefore, that the best bowler must also be the best batsman?

Yes, Socrates; you are undoubtedly right.

And something more seems to follow, I said.

What is that? he asked.

We admitted, I think, that the best bowler, being the best at taking wickets, was also the best at guarding or keeping them?

We did.

But he who keeps the wickets is the wicket-keeper, is he not?

Yes.

And he who is best at keeping the wickets is the best wicket-keeper?

Certainly.

We must conclude, then, that the best bowler is also the best wicket-keeper.

Indeed we must.

Not only, therefore, was I right in saying that the Daemon is the best batsman; but I may now add that he is also the best wicket-keeper.

Yes, you are quite justified.

At this point Athletes, who had evidently been listening with great impatience to our argument, suddenly turned round upon me like a wild beast, and seemed about to tear me in pieces; what nonsense you are talking, Socrates! he exclaimed with an oath—why, the Daemon never took the wickets in his life; and, as for his being a good bat, it is only very rarely that he makes a run.

Do not be angry with me, said I, as though terri- fied; I am only anxious to learn. Let me therefore take your statements singly. Do you say that the Daemon never took the wickets in his life?

I do.

And yet just now you declared that in this very match he is taking all the wickets! You do not treat me fairly; you are making fun of me.

Hereupon my friend only became more angry than ever; and made use of some very violent language. When he had quite recovered his temper, I continued. But I will forgive you that, I said, if you will treat me more kindly in future.

Instead of answering me, Athletes pointed to a young man in a many-coloured cap whose wicket the Daemon had just captured, and said somewhat scornfully: Of course they can do nothing, if they have two minds about every ball, like that fellow there?

You hardly speak correctly, I replied; for surely nobody has two minds, least of all a gymnast; but I quite see what you mean. That unfortunate youth was indeed much perplexed; for while the spirited part of his soul was urging him to advance and strike the ball, the more timid or philosophical element counselled him to stand still, and play it gently; and not knowing which to obey he failed utterly and was bowled.

Yes, Socrates, he said; you are right for once.

Speaking generally, I think you will also agree with me, I said, that it is not advisable for the soul of the same man to be affected in relation to the same ball of the Daemon's, at the same time, in contrary ways, especially when the ball is very near him.

Right again, he said; a man so affected is bound to be out, for the Daemon is always on the wicket, being, I suppose, about the best bowler in the world.

Forgive me, my dear Athletes, I said, if I say I cannot agree with your last remark. The Daemon certainly bowls very straight, but I cannot call him a good bowler. What do you think, Agymnasticus? Am I right?

Probably you are, he replied, though I don't quite see how.

That I can soon show you, I said, if you will allow me. Let us again consider bowling, which we admitted to be an art, by the analogy of the other arts.

By all means, he said.

We see at once, I said, that each art as such considers not its own interest, but rather the interest of that which is the subject of it.

I do not quite understand, he said.

For instance, the art of medicine as such does not consider the interest of medicine, but the interest of the body ?

True, he said.

And the lawyer's art considers the interest not of the lawyer, but of his client ?

Certainly.

And the scout cares always not for his own interest, but for his master's ?

Invariably, he said; I think I see your meaning now.

Very well, I said; then whose interest should the bowler consider ? Who is the subject of the bowler's art ?

The bowled at, I suppose, he said.

Yes, I said; or, in other words, the batsman. It follows, then, that the bowler as such will consider the interests of the batsman, and will bowl such balls as will please him?

It does.

But what sort of balls will please the batsman most?

I have not the slightest idea, he said.

Well, I said; can you imagine anything more delightful for a batsman than a half-volley to the off?

No, I cannot, he replied.

Unless it be a full-pitch to leg.

Yes, perhaps we ought to make that exception.

It follows, then, that the bowler as such will bowl only half-volleys to the off and full-pitches to leg, and that he is the best bowler who bowls most of such balls.

That seems to me perfectly reasonable, he said.

Again, will a good bowler ever bowl a straight ball? Surely he will not; for by so doing he may perhaps strike the batsman's wicket, and so make the subject of his art worse than he was before instead of better—a thing which no true artist would ever do.

I quite agree, he said.

Verily, Agymnasticus, I said, glorious is the power
of the art of dialectic, which has brought us to such
a conclusion as this. Perhaps the wits will laugh at
us when we tell them that the best bowlers do not
bowl straight; but we shall speak our minds never-
theless, begging of these gentlemen for once in their
life to be serious. And when one of these cunning
and deceptive bowlers like the Daemon here comes
to our city and wishes to make a public display of his
talents, shall we allow him to do so, or think of ad-
mitting him to our eleven?

Certainly not, he said.

No, I said, we certainly shall not; but we shall tell
him that he may be a very good batsman and a very
good wicket-keeper, but that he is certainly not a
good bowler, as we have already proved.

Quite so.

And if he is still unconvinced, we might add another
argument, I think.

What is that? he asked.

He would admit, I suppose, that that which par-
takes of reality and has the faculty of knowledge
corresponding to it, is of a superior nature to that
which is unreal and is only the subject of opinion or
ignorance?

Of course he would.

Now the subject-matter of ignorance is not-being, is it not?

Yes, he said.

And what kind of not-being are the batsmen and bowler concerned with? The no-ball, is it not?

Certainly.

Of the no-ball, then, the batsman is entirely ignorant?

Yes.

Similarly, he is in a state of opinion with regard to those balls which seem to roll about midway between being and not-being, and to play double, as the saying is, creating but a confused blur of sensation which the perplexed soul cannot discriminate.

Yes, he said; and it is in this state of mind that our young men seem to be to-day with respect to the Daemon's bowling.

Yes, I said; and he very rarely bowls the best and most real kind of ball—that, I mean, of which the batsman can have perfect knowledge.

Very rarely indeed, he said.

We should tell him then, that, as for the most part he bowls balls as to which the batsman can only be in a state of opinion, and occasionally even no-balls of which they are bound to be ignorant, but very rarely the complete and perfect ball—the full-pitch and the like of which there is perfect knowledge, he is therefore not a good bowler.

If, then, he comes to our city, and wishes to be admitted to our Eleven, we will fall down and worship him as a sacred and admirable and charming person; but we must also tell him there is no place for him in our Eleven, for we prefer the simple honest bowler who considers the interests of the batsman and does not deceive him. And so having anointed the Daemon with myrrh, and set a garland upon his head, and perhaps entertained him at dinner, we shall send him away to another city. For we mean to employ only the simple honest bowler who considers the interest of the batsman and does not deceive him.

Here Athletes interrupted me, and said with a laugh (for he had now quite recovered his temper), I hope, Socrates, I may be allowed to play against your eleven of honest bowlers when you have made it up; it would be great fun. But I rather think, to use one of your own phrases, that, though the model of such an eleven may be laid up in heaven, we are not likely to see a copy of it on earth.

M

It was now my turn to be angry, so turning to Agymnasticus I told him it was time to go.

By all means, he said, for I was just thinking, Socrates, that my state of mind with respect to the subjects in which I am to be examined is rather one of opinion than of knowledge, and a little more study would do me no harm.

Probably not, I said; and taking him by the arm I led him away, leaving Athletes convulsed with laughter, and evidently thinking he had done something very wonderful.

C. T.

FRAGMENT OF A DIALOGUE

(With apologies to Mr. T. L. Peacock)

Between the eminent historians, Mr. Omnium Gatherum *and*
Mr. Hobtoaster, *and* Mr. Pitiable Pedant.

Mr. Om. Gath. You will find that modern Oxford regards these questions from a broader and more liberal point of view.

Mr. P. P. Be kind enough, my dear Omnium, to have compassion upon the infirmity of my understanding, and employ some other phrase. I have had the Endowment of Research from the broad point of view, and the Boards of Study from a broader point of view, and Female Education from the very broadest point of view, until, I must frankly own, amid this kaleidoscopic variety, I sometimes, perhaps irrationally, sigh for a fixed point of view. But pray continue with what you were saying.

Mr. Om. Gath. I was saying that we want for those who study Modern History a more satisfactory course than is afforded by the Classical Moderations. For the Final Honour School of Modern History

M 2

we require a previous course of training in Greek
and Latin authors——

Mr. P. P. Dear me, you surprise me!

Mr. Om. Gath. ——in order that our students
may acquire methodical habits of thought and precision, and facility of expression. The mass of facts
they have to master is great, the authorities they
must consult are numerous, and therefore they require previous practice in the selection, the arrange-
ment, and the analysis of materials. The study of
original authorities should be one of the most
valuable parts of the Modern History course, and
therefore the student must not be a novice in the
study and appreciation of the spirit and contents of
works written under different conditions of thought
and civilisation, and in a different language.

Mr. P. P. Most excellently put! I had scarcely
expected such a line of argument from you. Surely,
Hobtoaster, you must applaud sentiments so just,
expressed in language so refined. It is the very
spirit of classical study.

Mr. Hob. Certainly; but are not these advantages to be obtained under the present Honour
Classical Moderations?

Mr. Om. Gath. We are considering a special class

of men, too able to bring their proud spirits down to the level of Pass Moderations, but yet, whether from deficiency of scholarship or maturity of intellect, unable to take their place in the treadmill of Classical Moderations.

Mr. Hob. But if the training be so valuable these men should surely make an effort. They have not been sufficiently drilled in scholarship : let them then learn the drill. They have not proved the armour of scholarship : then let them march with the smooth stones from the brook of Bohn.

Mr. P. P. Gentlemen, gentlemen, a little more sobriety in the use of metaphor. What with tread-mills, and training, and drill, and brooks, I really ——. But pray go on. Let Omnium develop his scheme. The men you speak of, Omnium, have souls above Greek and Latin, and are deficient in scholarship, yet you wish them to obtain all the advantages of a long classical training within a limited period, and to receive first-class honours for their pains. It is a most devout hope, Omnium, but my sagacity has never yet discovered any way of getting a tree to grow without first planting it, or of becoming a man without having first been born into this miserable world. But pray continue.

Mr. Om. Gath. I, and those who think with me, regard this proposed Preliminary Honour Examination as a substantive portion of the Final Examination; we have therefore chosen a list of authors different to that selected for the Classical Moderations.

Mr. Hob. You have got off Latin prose, but the number of Classical books is much the same in both lists.   You have limited the amount of Homer, Cicero and Demosthenes; and Claudian, Ammianus and Sidonius have taken the place of Virgil, Horace and the Greek dramatists.

Mr. P. P. O admirable consummation ! the mountain has indeed laboured to some purpose.   Not one mouse only, but three.   You have provided admirably for those methodical habits of thought, that precision and that facility of expression on which you justly laid such stress.   The poets of Augustus yield to the panegyrist of Stilicho and the last of Rome's Latin historians, while the glories of the dramatists of Attica pale before the imperial splendours of Sidonius Apollinaris.

Mr. Om. Gath. He is indeed an admirable author. So also are Claudian and Ammianus Marcellinus. Strabo too is very tasty in parts.

Mr. P. P. If they had only written in either

Greek or Latin ! I must own that I prefer the purity of the Attic dialect even to the rich variety of the κοινή, and the diction of the Augustan age to the best efforts of the "infima Latinitas——"

Mr. Hob. Now, Pitiable, I must really protest. I am bound on this point to make common cause with Omnium. A truce to this pedantry. In modern Oxford we look at things from a far broader standpoint: we read the ancient authors for the sake of what they convey and not as a mere linguistic study, or a peg for grammatical disquisitions.

Mr. P. P. And yet linguistic study and grammatical analysis are perhaps an aid to those methodical habits of thought and that precision on which both you and Omnium justly lay such stress.

Mr. Hob. I will never admit it. Now take our present Classical Honour Moderations. Our students read, besides their special books, the poems of Homer and Virgil and the speeches of Demosthenes and Cicero——

Mr. P. P. Do they? It must be the Undergraduates who do so, because I have met some of their tutors who have not read all these.

Mr. Hob. ——And I am in favour of adding to

this list the Politics, Poetics, and Rhetoric of Aristotle —most valuable treatises you must admit—and the works of Caesar and Herodotus. We must read these works as literature and not as puzzles in language. We may not be minute or accurate grammarians——

Mr. P. P. Why, no !

Mr. Hob. (*continuing*) ——but we will be scholars in the sense in which Macaulay defined a scholar, as "a man who could read Greek and Latin with his feet on the hob."

Mr. P. P. Bless my soul, Hobtoaster, you don't really say so—"with his feet upon the hob?" And could Macaulay actually do this? I could too if I resolved to pass over all the hard passages

Leaving vocabular ghosts undisturbed in their Lexicon limbo,

and

Into the great might-have-been upsoaring sublime and ideal.

You rather remind me of the youth who believes that all grammarians, from Dionysius Thrax to Dr. Rutherford, only lived and wrote for the sake of tormenting boys. Take my word for it, Hobtoaster, without knowing your verbs or your particles or your constructions, or attending to grammatical analysis or the distinction between subject and predicate and object, you will make sorry work of your Greek and Latin, even "with your feet upon the hob." What has become of the methodical habits of thought and the power of accurate analysis on which you and Omnium justly laid such stress? Is this all the choice that is left me?

ἔνθεν γὰρ Σκύλλη, ἑτέρωθι δὲ δῖα Χάρυβδις

—a quotation which, I hope, I have made with some servile approach to grammatical accuracy. On the one side the Scylla of Macaulay with his feet upon the hob, and on the other the Charybdis of Omnium with his Sidonius Apollinaris.

Thanks Hobtoaster and gentle Omnium,
Thanks Omnium and gentle Hobtoaster.

Mr. Om. Gath. The most important, and to my mind final, argument has not yet been stated for my view of this matter, and that is, that this preliminary examination is a first step to the establishment of the great truth of the Unity of History which——

[*Exeunt, running at great speed, Mr. Pitiable Pedant and Mr. Hobtoaster.*]

Explicit Dialogus.

K.

YE ROYALL VISITE.

Nowe I shall tell ye of a greate mattere and let everie one that redeth these thinges think the higher of me, for I which write have seen the Kyng's Son. This same gracious Prince did visite Oxenforde the whiles I sojourned there, the occasion of which Honour to the Universitie I shall now set forth. There dwelt in this Citie certain doctors, learned in diverse strange Tonges, *Sanscrit* and *Arabian*, with the Dialects of *Indoostan* and *Cathaye*. These same desiring a place wherein they might get their learning the more privilie and teach it without let from any man, set to and bilded untoe themselves a lyttel house in a sweete corner, at the mingling of the Street of the Holie Well and the way which is called Broade, nigh untoe the Library of Master Bodlie. And when the bilding was nowe aboute half done there cometh the Kyng's Son to laye the Foundation. For in this Countrie the Kyng's Sons be no idle Roysterers, but all their joye and course of lyfe is to laye stones and bild houses : nor may any man bild

hym an house unlesse the Kyng's Son laye the first
stone. Onlie, if the Kyng's Son be distracted of
much Bissinesse, then may they begin, and anon he
cometh and putteth hym in a stone, and setteth seal
upon the bilding. Which is what was done here.
In this countrie alsoe be there two sortes of Masons,
and the mannere of the twain is this. The one be
laborious and swettie folk and are of none account,
but the others do no work and be held in much
honour: and because they do no work therefore be
they called Free Masons. These saye that theye
kepe certaine greate and dreade secrets the which if
common men should knowe the Devil would be let
loose upon the Earth. Alsoe they say that these
secrets be revealed untoe no man except they first
torture hym privilie, for the better ascertaining of
his Constancie, proddynge hym with heated pokeres
and frying hym over a gryllyng iron. But others
saye they be lyttel more than knaves, having no
secretes. And indeed as concerning the pokere I
myself am not over confident, for the Masons which
I beheld were all stoute men and whole.

Nowe on a certaine daye these fellowes were
gathered together on the toppe of that house with
great ladies and dignities, there being present alsoe

certaine men, Princes, of a swarthie colour wearing
raiment of gold and silver.   And none wotted who
these were, but the wiser sorte said they were
Sanscrits.   All being readie and my Lords the
Chauncellor and Vyce-Chauncellor being come to
their seats, there ascended the Masons conveying
the Kyng's Son amid much ioyeful booing and
cheering of the meaner sorte which were gathered
together belowe.   Alsoe certain yonge Clerkes
leaving their bookes made greate jollitie in the
windows of the houses round about.   But these
were lazie lads, and on the morrow were whipped
solemnly by my Lord the Vyce-Chauncellor for their
idlesse.   The Prince was a ful grave and semelie
man to look upon and was girt about with a fair
gold apron, and over hys shoulders he wore a red
Doctor's gown, as a sign of hys great learning.   He
then being sat down, up iumpes my Lord the Vyce-
Chauncellor and says me certaine lyttel psaumes :
alsoe he prayede somewhat.   And after the Singing
Men had sung an hymn, but faintlie, the Kyng's Son
being brought to the place where the stone was, and
having hung thereon a writing in bronze, bade one
praye.   Then the priest of the Free Masons prayede
to their gods : nowe the Masons have two gods : the

one is called Iabez and the other Boaz. When
this praying was ended my Lord the Prince
scattered graine, with good oil and wine upon
the stone and daubed it deftlie with mortere, and
under it he set a Bottel in an hole: and in the
Bottel (so told me one that saide he knewe) were
manie curious charmes: soap made of peares
for easy shaving, and a spelle whiche a certaine
cunning woman brought from Mexico for the better
adorning of olde haires, and a papere which is called
Ye Tymes, and is more soughte after in that countrye
than anye other: of thys papere one told me that it
is alsoe entitled Ye Pynqun. And when my Lord
the Prince had set the stone in hys place there was
given untoe hym the trowel wherewith he layede that
stone, being of silver and curiously carved. For the
Kyng's Son ever taketh with hym the trowel wherewith he layeth, and this is what is called the Kyng's
prerogatyve. Of these trowels he hath in hys Palace
fourtie and nine thousand, five hundrede and seventie-
three: so industrious is he. Then my Lord the Arch-
bishop essayed hys turn at prayer, if perchance he
should prevaile bettere than the reste; and after that
he was done the Clerkes sang again, this tyme the
National anthem, for soe they call this hymn for the

Kyng and Queene. Nowe it being lawe that all do uncover whiles this hymn is sung, and the wind then blowing freshly, there was great ducking and dabbing of heads and blowing about of grey haires, while one cries "Alack my bald pate, what a rheum will have me," and a second, "God save my wig for I think it is cleane gone," and a third cursed bitterlie. All being finished, the nobler sorte departed to eat with my Lord the Vyce-Chauncellor. And of this feaste I saye no more, for I might not entere, though my bellie pynched me sore ; but one may think what consumption of tortoys soupe was there, and of salmon fish cookede in a yellow messe, what bibbyng of wines and brandies. And in the evening, my Lord the Prince being returned, there went about the streetes many both of the Clerkes and of the Towne boyes, and brake one another's heades for ioye of the Kyng's Son's coming : for this is the way of that people when they be glad.

MENDAX.

THE NON-PLACET SOCIETY'S ANNUAL
DINNER, 1888.

MENU.

POTAGES.

Consommé du conseil hebdomadal.

Purée de nid de jument.

POISSONS.

Poisson d'Avril, sauce réactionnaire et cléricale.

Concierge marié (réchauffé) à la Clifton.

ENTRÉES.

Hachis de réputations perdues.

Langues modernes sautées.

Cervelle de spécialiste.

RÔTIS.

Épaule froide à la nouvelle école.

Pièce de résistance à Freeman.

LÉGUMES.

Choux-fleur du système-Parc.

Champignons à la rêve utopienne.

Pommes de terre aux sciences naturelles.

VOLAILLE.

Canard à la calamité nationale.

———

BORE'S HEAD.

———

ENTREMETS.

Trifle ill-considérée.

Compote de l'histoire unifiée.

———

Œufs à la Hatch.

Devilled Professors on toast.

———

Fromage.

———

Dessert.

———

Cigares Intimidads.

Cigarettes Flor fina de poésie professoriale.

Tabac Pelham noir.

The proceedings were private, but the following selection of Music is understood to have been performed during the evening :—

OVERTURE . . La Vie de Collège.

SONG . "A Bachelor once with his feet on the hob."

GAVOTTE . . Pas des réactionnaires.

SONG . . "Hey, nonny, nonny? non!"

FINALE . . Marche triomphale rétrograde.

———

God save the Vice-Chancellor.

L'ENVOY.

I⊤ is but rarely that those who, by no fault of their own, have from time to time become responsible for the conduct of this paper, have spoken of themselves. Editors have changed—so much may be admitted— but the qualities of each have been absorbed and assimilated in the vigorous process of organic growth : the transparent honesty of the first, the serene im-· peccability of the second, the sombre enthusiasm of the third, have been but manifestations of a force and an energy which has been developed, and not transformed, in the lofty indifferentism of the fourth or the suave integrity of the fifth. It is not only μουσική and γυμναστική, as those who founded the paper dreamt, that have for the first time been mated in Platonic union : Radicalism and Toryism, Specialism and Obscurantism, the varying and conflicting claims of Rowing and Football, Classicalism and Letto- Slavism, Archaeology and the Theatre,—all these, and other phases of thought and action, the *Magazine* has embraced as occasion offered, has nourished as long as convenience served, and has laid aside as the evanescence of public interest, or the rise of new excitement, seemed to suggest. Our achievements modesty forbids us to record ; and there are many things in which we have not been successful. We have assisted the Hebdomadal Council in the establishment of the Non-Placet Society, but the thoroughgoing and drastic reform of the former body must be left to our successors. We have discussed the affairs of the Bodleian ; it will be for others to set the Librarian high above the approaches of carping critics, and to convince sceptics, reasonable or unreasonable, of the merits of the subject-catalogue. Boats and teams, whether representing the University or the Colleges, have had the benefit of our advice : some of them have been unsuccessful, and in all the most important lines of life the University of Cambridge still maintains a creditable competition. Of criticism we have had our share : a judicial impartiality has been mistaken for aimless tergiversation ; sobriety of thought has been represented as the stagnation of dull minds ; we have been accused with equal force of athleticism and aestheticism, of veiled obscurity and brutal candour, of cynical ferocity and

sickly sentimentalism. If we have abstained from
personality, we have been asked for Attic salt; if we
have said scrimmages were tight, we have hurt the
honest forward more than if he had been bitten:
advanced thinkers have detected a want of wit in
our sermons, an absence of idealism in our occasional
verse. But of criticism the paths are many—the
voice of the *Magazine* is one, and of all editors alike
this much may be said :—they have never hesitated
to stand up for the right when they felt that public
opinion was with them, they have always protested
against the wrong when they saw it to be unpopular :
they have stated truth when they have happened to
know the facts, and have never hesitated to resort to
fiction when they have been convinced of its superior
validity; they have never employed the lumbering
and tedious methods of demonstration when they felt
that they could rely on the credulity of their readers ;
they have never asked for gratitude when they found
self-satisfaction the surer road to happiness ; their
merits have not met with formal recognition, but they
have not taken a blue.

www.ingramcontent.com/pod-product-compliance
Lightning Source LLC
Chambersburg PA
CBHW022351020726
47500CB00002B/227